Praise for

Beirut 2020:
Diary of the Collapse

"For anyone who knows Lebanon or is newly curious about it in light of recent events, Charif Majdalani's *Beirut 2020: Diary of the Collapse* is a brisk, stunningly vivid, crushing account of a country in the midst of total self-annihilation. It's a must-read for Lebanese abroad who've missed out on the events of the past two years in Beirut and in the country at large, and for expats and visitors, both past and future, who have long admired this beautiful and vexed country. Especially for those Lebanese who feel survivor's guilt as they watch the devastation from afar, it's a brutally honest account of what's happened, what keeps happening, and perhaps what has happened once and for all—in the most hopeful sense possible—to a place we cherish."

—Salma Abdelnour, author of *Jasmine and Fire: A Bittersweet Year in Beirut*

"Covid-19, the economic crisis, the bankruptcy of the government, and the devastating explosion at the Port of Beirut on August 4, 2020. This is the chronicle of surrender that we witness in slow motion as Lebanon descends into social, economic, and political ruin. This is the diary of a man passionate about his country, written with anger and heartbreaking eloquence. This is the testimony of the mind-boggling absurdities of everyday life set against their political and historical sweep. While in the background there is the hum of the electricity generator and the smell of gardenias. Majdalani is magnificent."
                                        —Kerry Young, author of *Pao*

"Charif Majdalani's *Beirut 2020: Diary of the Collapse* is the most important work of literature from a year of shared global tragedy. In astute and despairing prose, Majdalani shows us his beloved city's pain, as the beauty and resilience of Lebanon are smothered by a surreal and menacing culture of government corruption and political rot. And then comes the explosion on August 4 of some 2,750 tons of ammonium nitrate. Majdalani's account of the explosion and the days following is intimately personal and particular to Beirut's devastation. At the same time, in Majdalani's wisdom Beirut's tragedy becomes a global cry. The same forces of oligarchy, corruption, and deliberate incompetence threaten all of us with cascading collapses of climate and ecological systems."
            —Nathaniel Popkin, author of *To Reach the Spring:*
                            From Complicity to Consciousness
                                    in the Age of Eco-Crisis

"The author's hometown is falling apart. He watches with sorrow as life leaks from its body, drop by drop. Lebanon's capital, which had been, for decades, the living symbol of the Levant, of its cosmopolitan cultures, of its joie de vivre, has morphed into a symbol of devastation and hatred and madness. Charif Majdalani is a survivor who still finds in himself the elegance to smile and hope."

—Amin Maalouf, author of *The Crusades Through Arab Eyes* and *The Disoriented*

"A searing, emotional rollercoaster of a read that deftly illustrates the despair and desperation Lebanese people endure daily. Majdalani expertly captures the hopelessness that most if not all Lebanese feel. And yet he still manages to entertain the reader with his sharp and cynical commentary on the country's absurdities and injustices. As a Lebanese person myself, I felt like I was looking in the mirror as I read Majdalani's powerful and vivid words. I could not help but cry throughout. But I also felt less alone."

—Zahra Hankir, journalist and editor of *Our Women on the Ground: Essays by Arab Women Reporting from the Arab World*

"More than an invaluable testimony, Majdalani has written almost a vade mecum with a universal scope. A life lesson in complete humility in the face of tragedy." —*Le Point*

"Political reflections, from which the author's cold anger springs, intertwine with his doubts and fears for the future. In strokes shot through with humor and dark irony, he builds on the portrait of a chaotic, lurching daily life."

—*Le Monde*

"A searing text." —*Lire Magazine Littéraire*

"A book at once deeply affecting and very cognizant of history."

—France Inter, *L'heure bleue*

"In his remarkable *Beirut 2020: Diary of the Collapse*, author Charif Majdalani examines the raw wounds of his country."

—*La Vie*

"A book of rare acuity." —*Transfuge*

Beirut 2020:
Diary
of the
Collapse

ALSO BY CHARIF MAJDALANI

Moving the Palace

Beirut 2020: Diary of the Collapse

CHARIF MAJDALANI

Translated from the French
by Ruth Diver

OTHER PRESS
NEW YORK

Originally published in French as
Beyrouth 2020: Journal d'un effondrement in 2020
by Actes Sud, Arles, France
Copyright © Actes Sud, 2020
Translation copyright © Ruth Diver, 2021

Production editor: Yvonne E. Cárdenas
Text designer: Jennifer Daddio / Bookmark Design & Media Inc.
This book was set in Burin Sans and Horley Old Style
by Alpha Design & Composition of Pittsfield, NH

1 3 5 7 9 10 8 6 4 2

Library of Congress Cataloging-in-Publication Data
Names: Majdalani, Charif, 1960- author. | Diver, Ruth, translator.
Title: Beirut 2020 : diary of the collapse / Charif Majdalani ; translated from
the French by Ruth Diver.
Other titles: Beyrouth 2020. English
Description: New York : Other Press, 2021. | Originally published in French
as Beyrouth 2020: Journal d'un effondrement in 2020 by Actes Sud, Arles,
France—Title page verso.
Identifiers: LCCN 2021008274 (print) | LCCN 2021008275 (ebook) |
ISBN 9781635421781 (paperback) | ISBN 9781635421798 (ebook)
Subjects: LCSH: Majdalani, Charif, 1960-—Diaries. | Authors, Lebanese—
21st century—Diaries. | Industrial accidents—Lebanon—Beirut—
History—21st century. | Lebanon—History—21st century.
Classification: LCC PQ3979.3.M34 Z46 2021 (print) |
LCC PQ3979.3.M34 (ebook) | DDC 848/.912—dc23
LC record available at https://lccn.loc.gov/2021008274
LC ebook record available at https://lccn.loc.gov/2021008275

Lebanon:
The Lessons of Complexity

During a stay in Beirut for a writer's residency, a French author once declared that Lebanon condensed and summarized in itself all the problems of the modern world, and that if only one of these problems could be resolved in Lebanon, it could then serve as a model solution for the rest of the planet.

The problems this writer was referring to are certainly numerous, and cover issues such as governance, the relationship of citizens with the state, political tensions, the power of the banks, untrammeled liberalism, and the endemic corruption of the ruling classes. And in a wider sense, the writer was of course focusing on the question of multiculturalism, the mix and coexistence of religions and cultures—issues that are part of the very foundation of modern Lebanon and its government structure.

In the beginning, before it became the name of a modern nation-state, Lebanon was the name given to mountains in the eastern Mediterranean that were long celebrated in the Bible for their snow, their symbolic proximity to the divine, and especially their famed vast cedar forests. From the very beginning of the Christian era, these mountains served as a safe haven for all the religious minorities that were persecuted by the various imperial powers in the region or by other larger religious groups. The last pagans of antiquity went into hiding there until the sixth century. Then came the Monothelete Christians, called Maronites, fleeing the persecution of the Orthodox Byzantine Empire in the seventh century, then in the tenth and eleventh centuries the Shiite Muslim communities persecuted by the Sunni powers, and the sect of the Druzes persecuted by the Shiites. Much later would come the refugees fleeing countless conflicts: Armenians in 1915, White Russians from 1920 onward, Palestinians forced off their land in 1948, and finally, very recently, refugees from the wars in Syria and Iraq.

For centuries, the religious mosaic and cultural diversity thus introduced into the lands that would become Lebanon were more or less well managed by the central powers of the empires on which Lebanon and its neighbors depended. Of course, there were clashes and conflicts, but everything remained under the slightly manipulative control of the dominant powers, and notably, from the sixteenth to the beginning of the twentieth centuries, of the Ottoman Empire.

When that empire collapsed in 1918, victorious France and Great Britain divided up the Middle East. It was France that secured the mandate over Lebanon, thus fulfilling the wishes of part of its Christian population, which sought to place itself under French protection and to avoid British rule. It should be noted that the Christians had long felt closely connected to France. Many had adopted the French language and culture well before the period of the Mandate, and had dreamed of the French taking control of the country to rid them of the Ottoman occupation. This privileged relationship between the Christians of Lebanon and the French also explains why the Lebanese never felt any hostility toward France. In the Lebanese worldview, France was never seen as an occupying power, but rather as an ally. Only the highly ideological left-wing discourse of the 1970s attempted to represent France as a colonial power, which it never really was in Lebanon, despite some instances of very transient irregularities. In fact it was with the assistance of the Christians, and on their advice, that the French determined the current borders of Lebanon in 1920: they adjoined a long band of coastline and the interior plain of Beqaa to the original Lebanon Mountains, along with the northernmost part of Galilee in the south. The overriding aim was to unite as many regions as possible where the inhabitants were Christian. The Maronites, the Eastern-rite Catholics and Greek

Orthodox communities actively worked toward the creation of the new nation in its present form, and considered it to have been founded for them alone, even though part of its population was Muslim or Druze. During a relatively soft Mandate that barely lasted twenty-five years, the French successfully managed the antagonisms between the various communities. But when Lebanon acquired independence in 1945, the foundations for discord were already laid, notably regarding the definition of the country's identity. The Christians still felt closely connected to the West, the Muslims for their part felt they belonged more to the Arab world. Nevertheless, the two communities both demanded and obtained independence together, then found a way of avoiding conflict by decreeing that the new Lebanon was not a Western country, but nor did it belong to the Arab world. This was the famous affirmation of national identity by a double negative.

This peculiar identity could undoubtedly be considered as the source of all the conflicts to come, but it also proved to be Lebanon's defining characteristic for many years: a nation straddling the great cultures of the East and the West, a crossroads, a herald of coexistence, openness, cultural exchange and integration. For the thirty years from 1945 to 1975, despite a few minor jolts, Lebanon also figured as something of an exception among its neighbors. It was the only country in the region not to fall prey to a nationalist military dictatorship, like Egypt under Nasser and Iraq or Syria under the Baath parties. It was the only democracy of the Arab world, and one of very few in what was then called the third world.

It also developed a liberal economy which has endured to this day, within a region entirely dominated by so-called socialist models—models which, in Nasser's Egypt and in Syria and Iraq, led to disastrous nationalizations, to the disappearance of their middle classes and the impoverishment of their populations. Lebanon thus lived for thirty years in unbelievable opulence and enjoyed exceptional cultural and economic vitality.

It now seems clear that it was precisely because of the diversity of its population and the complexity of its human institutions that Lebanon avoided dictatorship and the so-called socialist models that beset the rest of the Arab world between 1950 and 1975. Religious affiliation, which in Lebanon is more cultural than strictly faith-based, underpinned all political relationships and balances. This was made manifest in the strangest political system imaginable, called "confessionalism." All government posts were allocated approximately equally between religious communities. Every single employment position in the public sector, from the highest level in a ministry to its lowest echelons, was reserved for one or another community, depending on its presumed importance. The president of the republic had to be a Maronite Christian, the prime minister a Sunni Muslim, and so on. This political system prevented any single community or individual from controlling the government, and averted any possibility of hegemony or coups.

All this nevertheless created something like an oligarchic system, where the political leaders were systematically elected from the most important family clans within the large religious groups. They ruled the country collegially, on the basis of elections where the focus was always on the interests of the various religious communities, rather than on political issues. And yet the social classes that divided society were strongly intercultural. A real middle class had arisen from both Muslim and Christian communities, in the face of wealthy upper classes that also recruited from various groups, just as the working classes had members from both sides of the religious divide. However, social identity and affiliation never produced true class consciousness, but were always dominated by a very strong sense of religious, cultural, and community affiliation.

All this explains why the tensions between the large religious groups remained very strong, in particular because the constitution created in 1945 implicitly gave more power to the roles reserved for Christians than to those accorded to Muslims. The Muslims demanded reforms, but the Christians, fearing for their status and survival and continuing to believe that Lebanon was created for them, refused. Moreover, the Christians held great fears at the prospect of the rise in power and militarization of the Palestinian organizations that had sprung from the refugee communities in Lebanon in 1948, and that started demanding to play a role in internal Lebanese politics in 1969 and 1970. The strategy of these organizations consisted in giving their support to Lebanese Muslims. Faced with this coalition of Islamic-Palestinian interests, the Lebanese Christians took fright and armed themselves in turn, leading inevitably to the Lebanese civil war, which lasted from 1975 to 1990.

This was indeed a civil war, in that most of the fighting was between the Lebanese people themselves, but it was also very much a foreign war, because the Palestinians, Syrians, and Israelis were also involved. In 1982 the Palestinian militias were forced out of Lebanon by the Israeli invasion. But the Israelis had to evacuate the invaded Lebanese territories and confine themselves to the southern border regions adjacent to Israel. This opened Lebanon's doors to the Syrians, who allied themselves with the Lebanese Muslims and Druzes, and with war chiefs such as the Druze Walid Jumblatt or the Shiite Nabih Berri, as well as with the Shiite Hezbollah organization, which was engaged in a war with Israel in the regions it still occupied. For their part, the Christians resisted the Syrians for years, under the command of men such as Bashir Gemayel and Samir Geagea. In 1989, the reckless and unruly Christian general Michel Aoun took it into his head to unite the Christian ranks, and threw himself into devastating wars against his rivals on the same side, notably Samir Geagea, which led to the collapse of the Christian camp in 1990 and to the entire country falling to Syrian control.

This marked the end of the civil war and the start of what is called the second Lebanese republic, which is divided into two eras. In the first, from 1990 to 2005, Syria dominated the country and its ruling class. The Muslim or Druze war chiefs, Jumblatt, Berri, along with the Hezbollah leaders, but also the less powerful Christian leaders who had pledged allegiance to the Syrians, all took over the controls. The other Christian leaders, such as Geagea and Aoun, found themselves respectively either in prison or in exile. The allocation of posts along religious lines was reinstated during this period, but with a notable difference: the dominant positions were given to Muslims and no longer to Christians.

But the main issue was that the war chiefs–turned–political leaders seized control of the government and public sector, in concert with the generals of the Syrian occupying forces, and together they developed a system of governance that was entirely based on clientelistic mafia practices. They took advantage of the huge public works program for the reconstruction of the country, and of the bountiful financial manna this generated, to shamelessly enrich themselves and to entrench corruption as a system of government and a way of life, with the culpable consent of a powerful caste of arrogant bankers. Nevertheless, this was the beginning of thirty years of renewed opulence, euphoria, creativity, and vitality, when the population shamefully closed their eyes to the actions of this noxious political class.

In 2005, the Sunni prime minister Rafic Hariri, the only politician who was not a former war chief and who showed himself to be extremely hostile to the Syrian control of the country, was assassinated by the Syrians with the help of Hezbollah. This sparked a huge insurrection, which forced the Syrians to withdraw. Those previously banished (Michel Aoun) or who were political prisoners (Samir Geagea) returned. But former allies of Syria, such as Berri, Jumblatt, and the Hezbollah chiefs, managed to stay in power. New alliances sprang up between them and those who had returned, which led to the persistence of the same clientelism and corruption in political practices as under the occupation. This finally brought about the collapse of the country in 2020—a disaster which the present diary documents from day to day.

Despite this tormented history, Lebanon really had been, and perhaps could still be, a laboratory for some important political and social experiments. The first of these experiments is the management of multiculturalism and religious coexistence, which have endured despite violent convulsions, and lead every day to new forms of acculturation and cultural diversity. This small country has also been the laboratory where the processes of transforming family, clan, and community affiliation into a sense of citizenship are repeated on a daily basis. In other words, it is like a small-scale reenactment under a bell jar of the very genesis of any democracy.

Unfortunately these experiments have been slow to be reflected in political practice. They have suffered from being subverted or misappropriated by the ruling class, whose poor governance, corruption, and clientelization of the citizenry on the basis of community affiliation might also serve as a test case. The crisis in Lebanon in 2020 showed the dangers resulting from hyperliberal economic policies and the absence of any regulatory authority or control over the country's social or economic life, which have turned political leaders into mafia bosses in their dealings with the nation's citizens. The Lebanese people were forced to endure this hyperliberalism and the transformation of the public sector into a mafialike structure. They were obliged, day in and day out, to invent original forms of social and civic regulation and transaction, in the absence of any higher authority doing so. For several decades, they thought that this might also serve as a model, before they understood that a world where the banks and the super-wealthy seek to manage the life of ordinary citizens by depriving them of any official recourse to government was a complete disaster on all levels—be it social, economic, urban, or ecological. In this way as well, Lebanon's recent history and collapse might serve as a forewarning and alarm bell for the entire planet.

Ch. M.

Beirut 2020:
Diary
of the
Collapse

W e walked over to the olive trees, he and I. There were
three of them, and some little holm oaks. On the hori-
zon, to the east and the south, you could see mountain ridges,
and in the two other directions it was so wide that you couldn't
make out the boundary of the plot. The fellow had offered me
another one, with a sea view, and I had replied that I didn't
care. I can look at the sea often enough, every day at home, and
if I'm going to be in the mountains I might as well gaze up at
the peaks and the canopy of sky above them, with its ballet of
stars at night. I don't think he understood a word I was saying.
He was strapped into a kind of vest, with a buttoned-up shirt

underneath it, although it was already starting to get hot. When we got past the olive trees, walking through the dry grass that sometimes covered the remains of hardened furrows, toward a little tumbledown shack that I'd like to have rebuilt, he asked me if I could possibly pay him in cash. I burst out laughing and asked him how he thought I could get hold of dollars in cash. He didn't comment. We had agreed on payment by check. He was just trying his luck. A few days ago, I asked Jad why landowners would ever sell their assets for cashier's checks, and he replied that it's usually because they have debts they need to repay as soon as possible, before the complete collapse of the pound. As for me, I want my every last penny out of the bank.

When I got home, Mariam announced that the washing machine was making a weird noise. And indeed, the noise was disturbing—a kind of regular clacking, almost rhythmical, to the beat of the rotating drum. I had actually just gotten it repaired a few days ago, the day before yesterday in fact. So I called the repairman, who didn't answer, of course. These details of daily life which are out of our control are frustrating and make me angry. It's easy to get angry these days.

On social media it's always the same thing, inexhaustible, ad nauseam: economic collapse, the bankruptcy of the country, capital control, exchange rates, the pound in free fall, inflation, and penury lying in wait for us all.

2

We couldn't find a table at any of the pub~~~ Badaro Street. Only two of them are shut. The others are packed. In the end Marylin, the manager of Super Vega, found us a table for four, and the six of us squeezed in together. Social distancing is sometimes a purely theoretical notion. The music was pleasant and there was a group of young women at the next table over who were screeching with laughter. One of them was trying to get her handbag off the back of her chair, which was almost stuck to Pierre's, and she elbowed my margarita glass, spilling it all over me. She stood up, wanted to apologize, was about to dab my shirt with a napkin, but then stopped short when she realized this might be taken the wrong way. We laughed about it, and she often turned around with open curiosity over the course of the evening, sharing our conversation and laughing at our jokes or Joy's puns. We spoke to her a few times, inviting her to turn around completely, which she eventually did. Our table and the one she was sharing with her friends gradually became a single table. One of her friends told us that she had been living in France but then decided to come home for good. She had sold the only asset she owned in order to do so—an apartment in Paris. She had been planning to start a small business here with the money. But it was now inaccessible, and she had the feeling that she didn't own anything anymore, just like most of us here. It almost made her laugh. When she found out that Nayla, my wife, is a psychotherapist, she wanted to know whether it was normal that she didn't feel much anxiety at the thought of having lost everything, and that all she'd been doing was cooking—for example, in the last few days she had been experimenting with all sorts of new and different ways to use sumac, as a seasoning for fried eggs, of course, but also braised sturgeon and ray wings.

"Where do you manage to find ray wings these days?" Pierre asked, as dumbfounded as the rest of us.

"I don't," she replied. "I make virtual recipes."

3

July 1

I spend my day running from one bank to the other, converting dollars into pounds at the official exchange rate, then comparing that to the banks' rates, then to the changers', then to the black market rate, doing calculations, planning my expenses half in checks and half in cash, going by the changers' rates or the black market, before getting completely muddled and giving up on the whole thing. My wife said the other day that if the entire population could put to better use just a fraction of the energy that it now spends struggling out of the trap set by our broke government and failing banks, then the country could be back on its feet within forty-eight hours.

4

The economic machine is breaking down, retail businesses are almost bankrupt, and yet the city has been seized by a frenzy of activity since this morning, just like in the glory days of its suddenly vanished opulence. The gridlock is no worse than it was back then, even though the traffic lights are out because of the electricity shortages. And where the lights are actually working, police officers are controlling traffic and encouraging drivers to ignore them, directing everyone to move at the same time with grand, raging gestures, as if they were vengefully making a point of reminding us that order no longer reigns, so why should anyone even bother respecting these last damned surviving traffic lights. The drivers are astonished. Some, like me, resist, under the officers' resentful eyes. They seem aware and ashamed that they have become representatives of the general chaos and the failure of the state, and are going above and beyond what's actually necessary, as if they were furiously smashing a prized object to pieces to punish themselves for having carelessly chipped it. I talked to my wife about this when I got home, she didn't seem to care about the feelings I was ascribing to the traffic officers. She doesn't like them and even before the economic crisis she thought that they actually tend to be the cause of the gridlock rather than anything else, that they always complicate any situation they are in, that city traffic is like a natural process, it always ends up regulating itself, and that human intervention only disturbs it and makes it more complicated.

5

July 2

There is something fanciful about chance, something tragic even. It was exactly one hundred years ago, in 1920, that the nation of Lebanon was founded. One can only wonder at the irony of fate that brought a country to its ruin on the same date as its birth, at the very moment when its centennial is about to be celebrated. How far back should I go, in those hundred years, to trace the genealogy of this disaster?

6

ebanon, the arrogant little Switzerland that claimed to be the heir of an ancient or even biblical nation, collapsed for the first time in 1975, after thirty years that tend to be idealized today. In fact they were thirty years of struggle, conflict, and undeclared wars to establish the country's identity. The Christians considered it as rightfully theirs and as having been founded for them. They refused to share any real power with the Muslims, who demanded what they thought was their due, while aspiring to align the country with the grand Arabist and Nasserite plans. The Muslims allied themselves with the armed Palestinian organizations; the Christians saw this as an existential threat, armed themselves as well, and then the whole thing blew up.

Nowhere else do those "thirty glorious years" deserve their name more than in Lebanon at that time, despite all the discord. As much for their dates—1945–1975, that is, the thirty years of the first Lebanese Republic, which followed the twenty-five indolent years of the French Mandate—as for the heights of opulence that the country reached during that period. Beirut's cabarets and nightclubs were the most famous in all the Middle East. In those days, Dalida, Jacques Brel, and Louis Armstrong performed in the theaters and the Casino du Liban, while the monumental temples of Baalbek were the backdrop for performances of the Beethoven symphonies conducted by Otto Klemperer and of Franco Zeffirelli's production of Monteverdi's *The Coronation of Poppaea*. Jean-Paul Belmondo frolicked with Jean Seberg in the corridors of the Hôtel Phénicia, Louis Aragon stayed at the Hôtel Palmyra, spies from all over the globe held assignations at the famous bar in the Hôtel Saint-Georges designed by Jean Royère, while Oscar Niemeyer was busy building the Tripoli exhibition center inspired by the one in Brasília. But Brigitte Bardot was not well pleased with any of this, and decreed after a film shoot in Beirut that she was disappointed, that it was too Westernized for her taste. She probably expected to find camels, donkeys, and belly dancers around Moresque fountains. But no, people danced the twist and rock 'n' roll, waterskiing and miniskirts were all the rage, and this all reached its paroxysm at the beginning of the 1970s, just before the collapse. Meanwhile, on the outskirts of the city, pitched battles were being fought between the Palestinian militias and those of the Christian parties, and the government had no control over the south of the country. At the time we were like people living at the foot of a volcano, cultivating our fertile land, working hard to get rich, enjoying the good times, while hearing the regular roars from the belly of the earth, feeling the tremors under our feet, and paying no heed, just shrugging and pretending that it had always been this way and will be for a long time yet. Until the day it was all gone.

7

The outbreak of the civil war in 1975 came like the reck-oning of all the accounts and miscounts of that first Lebanese Republic. In the early years of the conflict, the militias were fighting with something almost like popular consent: their members were considered as heroes sacrific-ing their futures and their lives for the common good or a worthy ideal, whether this was the defense of Lebanese iden-tity or the exaltation of its Arab greatness. But this didn't last. The Syrian interventions from 1979 onward, then the Israeli ones in 1982 and the overturning of the chessboard that they led to, and especially the extended duration of the conflict, inevitably transformed the first armed groups into regular militias, then into quasi-professional armies. The behavior of the combatants changed too, and many of the first volunteers on the battlefields decided not to continue fighting because of the erosion of their original ideals. The enthusiastic young men from the beginning of the conflict were gradually replaced by career soldiers of sorts. The osmosis with the general population slackened, then a real hostility toward the militias started to appear on both sides, and in the same way in both camps, without this hostility coming into plain sight. Just as naturally, the historical politicians, the leaders of the first republic who were also the main proponents of the war—Pierre Gemayel, Camille Chamoun, Kamal Jumblatt, or Saeb Salam—were gradually overwhelmed or eliminated, then supplanted by a new generation, not of politicians anymore but of warlords: Samir Geagea, Elie Hobeika, Walid Jumblatt, or Nabih Berri. Their various militias and the countless clients that prospered in their orbit bled the country dry for a decade, through racketeering, trafficking scams, and the control of the half-bankrupted public infrastructure, notably the ports and airports. Which explains why the rise of General Michel Aoun, the commander in chief of what was left of the legalist army, made such a big impact, and why he generated so much enthusiasm. This reckless and clumsy braggart promised, in grand waffling speeches, to cleanse Lebanon of its militias, then to rid it of the Syrian presence. But after bloody and pointless battles, instead of succeeding he managed only to complete the ruin of the country, to unite all the militias against him alongside the Syrians, and to allow the Syrians to get rid of him and gain control over the whole country by ending the war by decree.

8

July 3

A few days ago, my daughter Saria got her driver's license in the most absurd circumstances: she couldn't sit the written test because of the lack of electricity in the examination center. She practices every day, driving me around on my various errands. She manages very well with the confusion caused by the missing traffic lights and the bizarre attitude of the police officers, but dreads the tunnel going down to the waterfront, which is plunged in perilously opaque darkness because of the failed electricity supply. Sometimes as we pass by, I point out a few ridiculous details of what is now our daily life, and yesterday, in fact, as we drove past a large bank, there was an incredible barricade surrounding it like a stronghold. She asks me questions about the situation, about her future, and whether there is any chance we would let her go abroad next year so she can continue her studies, as a number of her friends are doing. The dreams that young people like her have of leaving, even though they were attached to the country until only recently, are the topic of some of our most distressing and awkward conversations.

But yesterday, we were talking about something else. At her request, I had just explained a few complex issues from our recent history to her, notably the civil war, and she surprised me by declaring that in fact, to summarize it all, this long and complex war between the Lebanese people had actually been won by . . . the Syrians. I had a good laugh about this at the time, and even conceded that this singular paradox did contain the whole truth. At the end of the armed conflict, those who came out the winners were, in each camp, those who were the closest to the Syrians or had backed them or sought their support at one stage or another. Hobeika, Berri, Jumblatt, or the Hezbollah chiefs, those "new" men who had already bankrupted the country during the conflict, would be able to share out the fabulous cake of its reconstruction, on the condition that they delivered a portion of it to the Syrian military leaders. After granting themselves an amnesty during a memorable vote in the first postwar Parliament, they began the installation of a vast network of control of the new state, in collusion with their old wartime chiefs of staff and the many clients gathered around them.

9

The second collapse was the inescapable result of the very principles of the second republic, and the mutation of warlords into "politicians." Right from the start, in the euphoria of the return to peace and the expectation of fabulous opulence, the tentacles of a gigantic system of siphoning funds allocated to the country's reconstruction were efficiently put in place. The mechanisms of dubious contracts, institutional racketeering, insider trading, fake invoicing, corruption, and complicity were brought up to operational speed very quickly at all levels of the state sector, which was overhauled for the sole purpose of enriching the people colonizing the country or those who had become its foreign masters. Useless construction sites sprang up, giving the impression of a beehive at work, slush funds became routine, along with favors and kickbacks, percentage deals, shared projects, fictitious jobs, and the clientelization of local communities.

The only real newcomer among the converted warlords at that time was the businessman Rafic Hariri, who was made prime minister after an agreement sealed between the Saudis (the financial backers of the reconstruction) and the Syrians (the keepers of the peace and unofficial occupiers of Lebanon). He arrived on the scene with genuine ambitions to rebuild the country, despite his questionable taste in urban planning that nearly transformed Beirut into a kind of megalopolis like those in the Gulf emirates. I don't know how much he allowed to happen, how much he was forced to do. He apparently used rather undemocratic means to strip the owners of the city center of their properties, granted himself a few privileges and off-book accounts, and plunged Lebanon into debt. More importantly, he was forced to work alongside the old Syrian-backed warlords who were now his peers, and to reluctantly offer them high-ranking sinecures in public office and astronomical payments for tender contracts. But even that was not enough, he was still not considered sufficiently docile. His assassination in 2005 provoked what was— although it is rarely described as such—the first real Arab revolution. Millions of Lebanese people in the streets expelled the Syrian occupiers from the country. Our naive belief at the time was that we were getting rid of those responsible for the widespread corruption undermining the government, that everything was going to be fine from then on, and that this second republic would serve its citizens at last. The enemies of Syria came out of the shadows, Aoun the braggart returned, and his followers saw this as the second coming of the Messiah, or of de Gaulle after the Occupation. Alas, politicians of all persuasions—newcomers as well as former allies of Syria who had kept their positions—renewed their old alliances or created new ones that had no other object but to preserve the oligarchy's control of the government, which continued to be profitable, extremely profitable.

10

All this lasted for thirty years. Maybe there is a riddle to be solved in the dates that define this country's history. Because thirty years, from 1945 to 1975, is also the time it took for the first republic to collapse. Another thirty glorious years, from 1990 to 2020, duplicated the preceding ones. Beirut became the party town and center of nightlife for the entire Middle East again, and maybe even of the entire Mediterranean. You would see more Porsches and Maseratis here than in Beverly Hills. It was a good place to be rich, but you could also become rich in art and design just as well as in business or real estate, and the banks offered such mind-boggling interest rates that it was an El Dorado for annuitants. Nothing was produced anymore, agriculture was abandoned, industry was nonexistent, people lived on imports, and the government decided to borrow US dollars from the local banks at absurd rates, in order to finance large-scale projects. The debt reached thirty billion, then forty, then fifty, and the interest alone was higher than the GDP. But Roberto Alagna was singing at Beiteddine, Placido Domingo at Baalbek, and the Miss Europe contest was held in Lebanon. Once again, we were dancing at the foot of a volcano whose threatening roars everyone refused to hear, or on the edge of a precipice into which we finally fell.

II

July 4

The repairman came to have a look at the washing machine. He admitted it was making a strange noise, opened it up, and there, to his surprise, he found an enormous screwdriver he had left inside it, which was what was causing the infernal clacking in time with the drum's rotation. He laughed and told me about a cousin of his who had a scalpel left in his stomach by a surgeon. Then he added that I was lucky, because if I'd had to buy a spare part it would have cost me the same amount as I would have paid six months ago for two whole new washing machines, maybe even three. I'm tired of all the never-ending images my compatriots use to illustrate inflation and the devaluation of the currency. But I played along, and even added my bit. I told him that a little earlier at the bank, for the first time I had seen a guy carrying two enormous plastic supermarket bags stuffed full of bundles of Lebanese banknotes.

12

This afternoon, as I was coming home from taking my son Nadim to visit one of his French friends who is returning to his country for good, I found myself in the middle of a demonstration of Sudanese people protesting the apathy of their embassy and its unwillingness to repatriate them. Most of them no longer have any work, or are earning only a pittance because of the devaluation. They suddenly appeared, several hundred of them, surrounding the cars in the intersection not far from their embassy. I recognized those called the Arabs, but also the towering Dinka from the South, and men from Darfur. It was quite strange. Apparently there are helpless young women sleeping on the sidewalk in front of the Ethiopian embassy, waiting to be repatriated because they were laid off or no longer want to work for so little they can't send money home.

When I got home, I observed my Sri Lankan building supervisor. He was standing in the middle of the little garden in front of the building, which he tends with meticulous care. He has nurtured the gardenias and hibiscuses back to vigor, and skillfully pruned the loquat trees. Anytime a plant is ailing on our balcony, we give it to him and a few days later, we find it thriving again. This morning he was looking after the rosebushes. He made me think of Professor Calculus and his white roses. Or even—with his indifference to turmoil, as his salary dwindles away to nothing and his future becomes even more precarious—of those Persian poets tending their rose gardens as the Mongol hordes were preparing to swarm into Isfahan and Tabriz.

13

We were late leaving Super Vega tonight, my wife and I. Nayla, who is always cheerful in the evening, was singing songs from her eccentric French repertoire from the 1930s. All along the street, the pubs looked like great islands of light spreading to the edge of the sidewalks, erupting with babble and laughter. But once you walked past the last of them, it was like leaving an ancient town, beyond which there is only forest—pitch black. There has been no electricity at all for a few days now. When you listen carefully, you notice that the rumbling of generators fills the night to its very depths.

You get used to it, it becomes part of the texture of darkness. Some generators stop at midnight, some don't. In any case, from midnight onward the streets become bottomless canyons, black ink punctuated by the red taillights of the cars speeding by.

14

The collapse of the electricity sector is the most telling symbol of the complete failure of the state. For thirty years none of the successive governments has modernized the grid or reformed the administration of the sector as a whole, or even made any attempt to do so. And yet, plans were proposed and funds often made available, but never with the objective of resolving the industry's problems once and for all, but just of applying quick fixes while waiting for an agreement between the leaders of the various powers on how to divvy up this seemingly undividable cake. According to the figures in circulation, forty billion dollars apparently vanished into the construction of power plants later found to be inoperable, as well as into the nontransparent importation of electricity from Syria and the leasing of mobile power plants from Turkey at uncontrollable prices. Forty billion dollars which could have given light to half of Africa, and which weren't enough, in thirty years, to offer more than a few miserable hours of electricity a day to a country as small as Lebanon. In the meantime, of course, people had to come up with a solution. This explains why a private market of neighborhood generators supplying homes and businesses gradually developed. The height of absurdity was reached in 2019, when one of the long series of governments decided that it should take control of these private enterprises. In other words, a government started to regulate and tax an illegal service set up as a stopgap for its own deficiencies. It was a kind of recognition of its own failures caused by stupidity or cynicism, and a way to use them to fill the public coffers emptied by these same failures.

And so for a few days now the electricity supply has completely dried up. The money is gone and getting a loan to buy fuel oil is now impossible. Whenever the relevant authorities finally acquire any, it vanishes. "We're not sure where the fuel that we are buying is going," says the astonished minister in charge. In other words, in the midst of the crisis, another few tens of millions of dollars that were found by scraping the bottom of the coffers have evaporated—again.

15

July 6

In the late afternoon, I was caught up in a huge traffic jam on my way home from seeing the lawyer with whom I'm working on the contract to buy that plot of land in the mountains. The driver of a car moving at walking pace to my left was vehemently discussing something, making grand gestures, talking to three people who were sitting in the back, perhaps because of coronavirus. The driver had pulled down his mask to be more comfortable in his diatribe, or in the lively story he was telling—I couldn't hear what he was saying. At one point, he hit one of the levers by the steering wheel without realizing it and his windshield wipers started going back and forth at high speed, as if they had adopted the rhythm of his speech, or as if they were ironically keeping time under his nose. Obviously this reminded me of Jacques Tati. I was sure that the man's conversation was about the economic crisis, his money locked up at the bank, inflation, and Covid-19. That's all anyone ever talks about, all day, every day, at home, in offices, in taxis. Day before yesterday, Nadim asked us if it might be possible, for an hour at least, to talk about something else.

16

July 7

B ut then again, what can I really be sure of? All our gestures and now restricted activities are projected onto an infernal backdrop, with poverty increasing before our very eyes, mass layoffs, suicides, all continuously being shown to us, virtually, through social media, the rumor mill, or the press. The only real evidence I have that something is actually going on is the direct impact it has on my daily life. And that impact is palpable in my worry and anxiety, my mind being permanently occupied by catastrophic scenarios, sudden doubts about the validity of my choices in this situation, with our bank accounts emptied out because we spent everything on purchases or even investments that will be worth nothing in a few years, and so how do we now face our future and our children's future in this ruin of a country? As I sit on my terrace, writing these lines, facing the mountains, in the scent of gardenias and the gusts of July wind, I could almost believe that nothing has changed, that everything is the same as it was in other Julys past. The noise of cicadas in the trees and of a construction site in the distance are those of the world's eternal daily routine. Optimistic thoughts rise up from the depths to which I had pushed them down, and the temptation of denial arises again, that same denial that allowed us to live so cheerfully for thirty years. We're still going to the pub after all, still having dinner with friends, my wife has lots of work, my own salary hasn't changed, even if it's worth six times less than it was six months ago. But I just have to go out during the day to see the erosive effect of the recession, and this makes my black thoughts start to rise up again: the stores we pass that are usually open for business—those places that are part of our habitual environment even if we never set foot in them—are closed one day, then the next, then the day after that, before we finally understand that they will never re-open again; the young salespeople in the stores we do go into, the bank employees with whom we had built up an almost friendly relationship, all those people who make up a familiar world and who are no longer in their rightful place either, and will never reappear there because they have all been laid off. It feels like a bereavement, a muffled, almost muted bereavement, repetitive, exhausting.

17

remember the moment it all happened, at the beginning of last fall. There were already worryingly insistent rumors circulating about the government going bankrupt and possibly seizing all bank deposits. Then the suspicions gradually turned to the banks themselves. But it was like one of those distant catastrophes you read about in the newspaper and are sure will never reach you. The final outcome of thirty years of denial. Eventually I did go to the bank one morning, but feeling skeptical, unsure, unconsciously refusing to admit that the predicted disaster was actually upon us. At the counter, as usual, without any hesitation, with even something like amusement or certitude, I asked to withdraw what was hardly an exorbitant sum (six thousand dollars, I remember, three thousand from each of my children's savings accounts). I didn't need it, but it was just to reassure myself, to confirm that it was still possible. I was even expecting the teller's usual smile, and a momentary shared look of complicity to show that we were not duped, he and I, by the dangerous rumors circulating, and that money was still available, and in quantity, as per usual, of course. Yet, instead of all that, I heard the young guy reply with some embarrassment but an attempt to sound as natural as possible, as if letting me know about a little transient annoyance, a technical difficulty, a computer glitch or a mix-up with the cashier, that alas, this was not possible, six thousand dollars was a lot of money, he wouldn't be able to give me the total sum, he would prefer that I take it out in several withdrawals, spaced out if at all possible, and at that moment I understood that we really had entered into what until now I had refused to see as anything but a nasty fabrication.

18

n the beginning the bank customers, deprived of their money and confronted with the denial of their unassailable right to withdraw their money as they needed or saw fit, were sometimes incapable of understanding or listening to reason and flew into rages that were filmed by other customers and posted on social media. You can still watch these scenes, which filled our daily lives, on various activists' and protestors' Web sites. All day long, there were cries of powerless fury, threats against the employees, attacks on the offices of the branch managers, attempts at self-immolation by fire, then endless negotiations with retirees and desperate small-time savings holders, with mothers, farmers, laborers. Gradually the banks gave themselves an escape hatch by authorizing small withdrawals, only in local currency, at a rate that was higher than the official rate but lower by half than the black market rate, which is in fact the only real criterion of exchange. In other words, in every transaction, the citizens lost and are still losing half their money, either directly if they exchange it immediately, which is what all the business owners and shopkeepers who buy raw materials or products in US dollars have to do, or indirectly, since this situation means everything for sale has doubled in price.

19

According to the *Financial Times*, the *Economist*, and other specialist magazines and newspapers, over the last three decades the Lebanese banks have set up dizzying Ponzi schemes, those illegal financial mechanisms that consist in offering customers huge rates of interest, which are entirely and exclusively drawn from the deposits of the following customers, in other words without any investment policies whatsoever. The system works as long as there are depositors who entrust their money to the banks operating these kinds of scams, while never declaring them and lying to their customers. But as soon as the depositors are no longer there, the system cracks open, takes on water, and inevitably sinks. The catastrophe apparently started when the great monarchies of the Gulf no longer added to their prodigious accounts in Lebanese banks, then when international aid stopped flowing in because of the obvious corruption in political circles. The banks had also given huge loans to the government, which was then incapable of repaying them, since the borrowed money was never used for the public good, but systematically vanished into the black holes of shell companies and off-book accounts controlled by the men in power and their political clients. Then the whole banking system collapsed.

The same sources confirm that as soon as the first cracks could be heard, billions of dollars were taken out of private accounts, most of which were associated with fortunes created through corruption and self-serving business practices. Even after the banks forbade outgoing international transfers, trapping the deposits and savings of the least well-off customers, and while thousands of people were standing around the hostile tellers begging for one or two hundred dollars of their own money, six billion dollars were still being fraudulently sent to tax havens. No one will ever know whose money it was, or who authorized those withdrawals.

20

July 8

Today on the ridge of Mazraa, a large city council truck, a monstrous beast carrying a tank and perched on huge rotating brushes, was moving slowly and ceremoniously, spraying and sweeping circles on the edge of the sidewalk. Or, to be more accurate, on the edge of the old flowerbeds in the middle of the road where nothing has been planted for eons—one more piece of evidence of the incompetence or corruption of the municipal authorities. It reminded me of the first days of the civil war. We could hear machine gun fire not far from our home, and rumbling explosions would make the walls shudder every once in a while—a sign that there was fighting over by the Tayyouné roundabout, only a hundred yards away as the crow flies—but the night watchman was still doing his rounds through the neighborhood, walking past our windows in his uniform, with his old double-barreled shotgun and his whistle.

21

The peg of the Lebanese pound, and therefore the entire economy, to the US dollar and the dollarization of the economy that followed meant that for decades you could buy and sell in either one currency or the other, since the exchange rate between the two remained stable. But now, the many different exchange rates make daily life completely surreal. Schools, insurance, medications, gasoline, and even restaurants have stayed at the official, extremely low exchange rates from before the economic crisis. Everything else is at variable rates so that when you go into a store, you don't ask the price of the products for sale anymore, only the exchange rate at which they are offered. It is all so absurd that, now I come to think about it, I realize that I paid the price of a bottle of tequila for our house insurance, but that the purchase of a new computer monitor for my daughter is setting me back more than the yearly school fees for both her and her brother.

22

We had dinner on the terrace, with Nadine, Paula, and Camille. The last time we had a meal here together was almost a year ago, on the evening before the start of the revolution of October 17, which we expected would herald the end of the ruling political class. We often remember that evening, when we shared our skepticism about whether there would be a popular reaction to the imminent wreck. A few days earlier, huge wildfires in the mountains were blazing out of control, because the new Canadair water bombers the government had acquired the previous year had not been able to take off. After some stammering and absurd justifications, it transpired that the entire maintenance budget for these planes had vanished into thin air. No one responsible was held to account for this, but a week later, for a different and much more futile reason, the popular insurrection had started. That's not likely to happen now, although some of us here this evening think the embers are still smoldering under the ashes. A breeze wafts past from time to time, a crescent moon finer than a scimitar's blade seems to be resting in the branches of the araucaria tree just across from us, which I found out a few years ago from Pierre Michon is called a monkey puzzle tree, because its prickly branches make it difficult to climb. I reported this information to Jean Rolin, when we were sitting there late one evening with Christophe Boltanski and my wife. It was during the 2006 war, Rolin was in Beirut for *Le Nouvel Observateur* and his book on stray dogs, and Boltanski for *Libération*. A few hundred meters away were the borders of the southern suburbs and Hezbollah districts, which were plunged in total darkness, and made the illuminated terrace where we were sitting up late into the night seem like the last inhabited place on Earth before the fall of darkness and silence.

Tonight there is no war or destruction, but the lack of electricity conveys the same impression of profound gloom. And yet a singular streetlight is still burning inexplicably on the sidewalk below, casting splashes of purple, pink, red, and mauve from a huge bougainvillea into the darkness. The generators are thrumming away in the depths of the night, beneath the bursts of our voices in conversation. A beneficent gust of wind floats by, and then the voluptuous scent of the gardenias rises.

23

As I was coming home from dropping off Camille, who'd come on foot, I saw a demonstration at the end of the avenue that leads to the Ring Bridge. It's one of the meeting points for protestors. There weren't many of them, but it sometimes happens that some surge of anger suddenly brings thousands of people out onto the streets again after nightfall. The roads are blocked off, dumpsters are set alight. We were there last time, two weeks ago, my wife and I, just like every other time. It was a spontaneous gathering, which later spread to other parts of the country, and I was surprised once again, in the middle of the crowd with its flags and megaphones, to find the corncob and coffee seller with his miniature tinseled stall set up on the front of his motorbike. A few months earlier, when the huge nighttime protests ended in skirmishes with the police and the reserve troops of the speaker of Parliament, that salesman had stayed amongst it all, moving along with the charges of the riot police and the retreats of the demonstrators. And he wasn't the only one doing this. There was also a water seller, a pugnacious little boy who stood his ground even as the tear gas was raining down and the young people were running away with balaclavas completely covering their eyes and noses. When they regrouped to advance once more, the little boy sprang up again in the midst of the white smoke, the shouting, and gunshots, as if he were at a fun fair, or like an improbable little djinn, loaded down with his packs of small bottles and proclaiming throughout the general chaos, the artificial fog, and the battle atmosphere: "Cold water! Cold water! Who wants to buy some cold water?"

24

July 10

This morning at around eleven, on the square in front of the National Museum, there's a traffic jam caused by a gigantic crane parked there. It lifts up an ancient stele from the platform of an enormous truck, then sets it down in front of the museum doors, then lifts it up again, rotating it slowly and setting it down again next to another stele and a sarcophagus that have been displayed there for years as part of the urban decor. I don't know whether the National Museum is open or whether any museums have been allowed to reopen after lockdown. But I imagine they must be strangely deserted. The collections are sleeping in the silence of a necropolis, without a single visitor—all the objects, the evidence, the relics that have served to illustrate the national narrative, to develop the ideological basis for the country whose founding fathers could never have guessed that exactly one hundred years later that same narrative would become the expression of the most bitter and shameful failure.

I don't know whether the museums are open, but in other places there is nothing happening. The art galleries are no longer holding exhibitions, or very rarely, there are no music festivals, there will be no more book fairs, the publishers aren't publishing anything anymore. Nizar Hariri, who is the head of a sociology research program at my university, told me a few days ago that the Ministry of Education had opened a tender for printing the schoolbooks for next year's curriculum. It's usually a contract that printing presses fight over, because it guarantees the sale of at least a hundred thousand books. But this year, not one of them even put in a bid. They have no confidence in the ministry's promises of payment. There will be no schoolbooks next year. Or this year's will have to be reused.

Most of the founding fathers of modern Lebanon were poets, writers, lawyers. But they were also shrewd businessmen, fastidious bankers, readers of Victor Hugo and José-Maria de Heredia, but also of *Commerce du Levant*, the venerable and still informative economic magazine that was founded in their era. According to this week's issue of *Commerce du Levant*, more than two thousand businesses closed their doors this last month, two hundred pharmacies, as well as the famous international brands that are leaving the country for good, such as Adidas and Coca-Cola. The Carnegie Center, for its part, estimates that more than a thousand businesses have folded in the tourism sector alone, putting more than thirty thousand families into penury. The French Foreign Ministry estimates on the basis of independent studies that there have been four hundred thousand total layoffs so far, a figure which represents one-twelfth of the total population.

25

July 11

first thought that the sudden disappearance of all those anti-mosquito coils you burn to get rid of insects was linked to the general shortages in the supermarkets. Then Nayla made me realize that it probably had more to do with the fact that it was impossible for many households to use the usual devices that you plug into a power socket, since there is hardly ever any electricity at all in many neighborhoods, especially at night. So we're back to using the good old burning coils, which have now disappeared from the market because of high demand—collateral damage of the economic crisis, but also of the Covid-19 pandemic. For I am firmly convinced that the worldwide slump in industrial activity and the lower pollution levels that allowed nature to reboot during the three months of lockdown all over the world have given a new unexpected vigor to plants and insects.

And so now we are suddenly defenseless against the bugs. A few days ago we were having dinner with Gilbert Hage and his wife at their place, and Gilbert, who is always easygoing and good-natured, with the girth of Winston Churchill and a chewed cigar permanently hanging from his lips, disappeared for a moment inside the house, then came back into the garden where we were having our meal, holding one of those coils which he lit up with the end of his Partagás. I told him this was a strange thing to do. He retorted, with his usual offbeat and unpredictable humor, that these coils were now so exclusive that you couldn't possibly do them justice with a simple matchstick. I then told them how the smell of these strange green products, whose smoke rises slowly into the air like incense, had been part of my childhood, especially during my summers in the mountains. Everyone around the table seemed to have the same memory. Then I recalled reading in Gabriel García Márquez that in the West Indies they used to burn dried cowpats to get rid of mosquitoes. Gilbert said that the burning green coils were in fact made out of compressed cow dung, with an artificial fragrance. The economic crisis in Lebanon, I said to myself, has led to the not-so-fortuitous encounter, at the home of a great photographer, of Churchill and a coil of compressed cow dung.

26

For the thirty years of the second republic, one of the most coveted contracts was for trash collection, and even more so for the management of public dumpsites. Obviously the tender involved endless manipulations, nontransparent transactions, and clientelistic maneuvers. The dumpsites were finally awarded to someone close to the Hariri family— who has since become a billionaire, along with the rest of his entourage—who respected almost none of the terms of his contract, notably regarding the sorting and treatment of the waste material. The landfills turned into huge mountains of trash, cliffs of filth collapsing into the sea at several points along the coastline, with a smell that throughout the years has often spread all over the towns and the whole seacoast like the malevolent spirit of a power that is rotten to its core, while we go about our business, work, study, shop, or have parties on the rooftops and in the trendy nightclubs, some of which claim a certain cachet from being located right up next to these cursed mountains. All the alternative plans for burying the waste or building incinerators were abandoned because of conflicts of interest. Some people say this was no bad thing, because incinerators or burial projects would just have led to the theft of more millions of dollars, the construction of inoperable factories, or even greater calamities for the environment. In 2015 a popular uprising took the ruling political class to task for the first time, because of what was called the trash crisis. Those in power got away with it through covert repression, by infiltrating the protestors and ecological groups or those fighting corruption, and reduced the movement to silence. Everything went back to normal, the stink prevailed, but that didn't matter since the garbage was still earning millions of dollars.

A few years ago, a literary journal asked me to write a dystopia set in Lebanon or the Arab world. I came up with a story of widescale real estate speculation in Beirut, of which there has been so much in the last few years, of ultramodern skyscrapers and business centers built by the mafias connected to those in power on land reclaimed by compressing and dumping millions of tons of trash into the sea. A shadowy business world, covered in gold leaf and knee-deep in garbage.

27

July 13

We had dinner at Pierre and Nada's last night. There were twelve of us, which was probably too many for social distancing, but miraculously, the subject of the economic crisis didn't come up once throughout the whole evening, as if a benevolent genie were floating above us or we were graced with the presence at our table of the Homeric gods, those creatures who influence events with crude but effective stratagems, rendering the words of an Achaean leader inaudible during a banquet, or a Trojan fighter invisible in the midst of battle. We thus kept the country's collapse and our own anxieties at a distance, for the space of one evening. When the topic came up of the trash that hasn't been collected for a few days now, the gods of Olympus did their work and a former secondhand bookseller changed the subject by telling the story of how he sometimes bought huge stocks of books, hundreds and hundreds of volumes, some of which had no value whatsoever and he put into the closest dumpsters in his neighborhood, only to find them again a few days later, offered for sale by rag-and-bone traders who had picked them out. He then decided to dispose of those useless acquisitions in more distant garbage dumps, in other neighborhoods, but the books came back, inescapably, as if by sorcery, or like a practical joke played on him by some laughing god.

When the topic of Covid-19 came up, with the possibility of a new lockdown that would finish the job of ruining the country once and for all, the Olympian gods reacted just as effectively, and Pierre, without changing the subject, transported it elsewhere, telling us with a straight face how he knew who Patient Zero was, the guy who had carried it out of China, and that he had almost met him. It was a colleague of his who was working in Bergamo. The guy had traveled to Singapore, where he had had meetings with Chinese industrialists from Wuhan. When he got home to Italy, he had met with his company representatives from Mexico, Madrid, and Paris, whom he must have infected, and then they flew home and had more meetings. He had done the same in Bergamo— including spreading the virus to people who the next day would attend the notorious Atalanta-Valencia match—which is now considered the epicenter of the pandemic in Europe.

He was then supposed to fly to Dubai, where he had a meeting planned with Pierre, who was there at the time. But he had felt flu symptoms and canceled his trip at the last minute, greatly disappointing Pierre, who had thought him rather fickle and fragile to cancel a business trip just because of a little fever. If the meeting had taken place, it would have been Pierre who brought the virus into Lebanon, and not that pilgrim woman from Tehran.

For a few days now, the new Covid-19 case numbers have been rising steeply, and there are rumors that there will be a new lockdown. It's like a bowling game for all the businesses and retail, where the ball is thrown again and again with ghastly regularity until everything left standing is eliminated. Any business or retail store that managed to pull through the first period of the economic crisis, capital control, and the collapse of the markets, had to suffer another shock: enforced isolation and the complete shutdown of both internal and external trade. Those who came out of it unharmed are now fearing the new lockdown, which would be like the final assault, the coup de grâce.

28

July 14

The spontaneous protest movements are not subsiding. They are made up of shock troops of young, tirelessly mobilized activists, who are occupying the ministries and the public service offices, settling in with their masks and their slogans, demanding to meet the ministers or the department heads, essentially to insist they quit their positions because they are not discharging their duties honorably. The police responsible for security in public places are apathetic and leave the protestors to it, observing them, sympathizing sometimes. But the ministers and senior public servants are never even there, or abscond early, or scuttle away through the service exits.

29

July 15

This morning I was coming out of the office of a friend of mine who had offered to make her errand runner available for some of our administrative formalities around the purchase of the land in the mountains, when I saw a woman sitting on a large threadbare couch, in the shade of a dumpster, sorting parsley—parsley which, in contrast to the worn couch and the grubby dumpster, looked fresh and almost poignantly green. She was wearing a black dress, her head also in a black veil that covered her mouth. A Nawar, surely, one of those mysterious people some consider to be the Asian cousins of the Roma. Maybe she had tattoos on her arms, gold teeth, and piercing eyes, I couldn't tell. She was very busy with her bunches of parsley, enjoying the faded and tattered old couch while she had the chance, before a junk dealer would find it and chase her away to claim it. Nawar women are generally fortune-tellers, and many of their people are also beggars. But it's a fact that for a few years now they have been supplanted in the streets by a vast deployment of a new contingent. At every intersection, women, little boys, and old men have developed a whole economy of the outstretched palm. According to a study published in 2015 by Unicef, the ILO, and various NGOs, the overwhelming majority of these newcomers—who are even more numerous and just part of the urban landscape now—are of Syrian origin, driven away from their homes by war and violence. Children in rags as young as eight or nine, teenage boys, fourteen-year-old girls with babies in their arms, old women too—a whole insistent world, prowling, banging on car windows, simpering, pleading, or walking past full of contempt for your indifference. Many of them are born here, in abandoned building sites or squatters' rooms or on the street, and are therefore completely stateless, abandoned unto themselves, the fruit of broken relationships, displaced families, or shotgun marriages. Many of them are apparently also victims of exploitative mafia groups.

One evening a year ago, a little girl who was already a mother, holding her baby in her arms as she might have held a doll if she had been born under other skies, planted herself in front of my wife's car window, at a traffic light, on Bechara el-Khoury Avenue. My wife always keeps a few cookies and candies in reserve for this kind of situation, and bread too if possible. But the young beggar didn't want them, she asked her to get hold of some diapers for her instead. Taken aback at first, Nayla, who had Saria in the car with her, hesitated, then finally went to a pharmacy nearby. She found the beggar again thirty minutes later, delivered her order to her and took the opportunity to try to ask her where she was from. The little mother muttered something incomprehensible, then pointedly turned away without showing any gratitude or giving a satisfactory answer. But by then she had been joined and set upon by other girls just like her, all carrying infants and coveting her diapers.

A few months earlier, curiosity had prompted me to lower my car window and ask a teenage girl, at the intersection of Verdun and Tallet el Khayyat Streets, where she came from. She spontaneously replied, "Aleppo." I tried to find out more and asked which part of Aleppo. The young girl threw me an aggressive look, then went to beg from another car, without answering me, as if I had been very rude to her. These children obviously lie to hide a much more complicated origin than they are prepared to admit to, or they simply don't know where they come from, either because they arrived here when they were very small or because they were born here. The birth rate of this population is apparently staggering. The Lebanese government has never taken any interest in them, letting poverty, domestic violence, ignorance, and no doubt also drug use and prostitution flourish. Today in the general collapse, the fate of this enormous population already

abandoned to its own devices is difficult to imagine. The unruly young men who loiter, shout, and beg as if it's a game to
them seem to me to be ideal recruits for new gangs or militias.
The nightmare scenarios of the future are already locked in
place.

30

July 17

Since biblical times, Lebanon has been seen as a beacon by the peoples of the Orient, by invaders from the East as well as those living in desert oases or in Palestine or Mesopotamia. It was the only known mountainous region, whose summits were said to bring men closer to the gods, or to the one God, and of course there was snow and water and infinite verdant valleys, with cataracts hurtling off cliffs, and gorges where cold torrents flowed. This natural paradise with its abundance of water and greenery led Lebanon to be compared to Switzerland in the Romantic period. For most of the twentieth century it was still seen as a dreamland by tourists from all over the world, especially by the global Lebanese diaspora, whose nostalgia for the sweetness of life in their homeland transfigured its mountains into places of legend.

Snow, torrents, water in profusion, and eternal greenery: for many years these features of the landscape were leitmotifs of the national narrative. For decades it was repeated that water was Lebanon's oil, in other words its precious fortune—an inexhaustible fortune, what's more, unlike the neighbors' petroleum.

Except that now there is no more water, just as there is no more electricity. Of course this is not a new development, we're old friends with taps running dry. But if this occurred even during the time—now seen as blessed—of the first republic, that was because the government of the day had taken no real initiatives to avoid water shortages at the end of the summer. During the thirty years of the second republic, on the other hand, there were countless projects. Numerous dams were built, destroying the mountains, the natural sites and landscapes, laying waste to valleys, gorges, and arable land. Many of the dam reservoirs dried up, because of leakages due to faulty construction or inaccurate land surveying. Opinions on their usefulness vary, but what is beyond a doubt is that nothing is known about the billions of dollars that were spent on them, involving fake invoices, cooked books, and gigantic amounts of siphoned-off funds. According to all the hydrogeologists I've spoken to, there is not a single one of these projects that was costed lower than at least five times its real value, and all this for final results that were always below acceptable norms. This is how it goes in other areas as well: roads, bridges, public buildings. No documentation is ever demanded of the corrupt companies involved, which are always linked to politicians. As for the regulatory agencies, they receive spectacular bribes to close their eyes to the huge irregularities they find. Or if they wish to keep things legal, they are excluded from the public contract tendering process and reduced to bankruptcy.

This morning I saw the first water truck making a residential delivery. It was parked in front of a building on Trabaud Street, in Achrafieh. The hoses were stretched up onto the roof of the building, the pump's motor was whirring away, making an infernal racket. Nobody knows exactly where this private water sold without any legal authority comes from, or which aquifers are being pillaged with no scruples or oversight. But soon, with the summer coming on, this spectacle will be repeated in every street, for days on end—with, in the background of the picture, mountains rising up that were once the water reservoirs for the entire Middle East.

With the truck blocking Trabaud Street, I had to reverse out and take another route. Just before I started backing up, a passerby stopped in front of my open window and announced gravely that soon there would be no water at all, not just in this season every year, but all the time, because there would be no more fuel oil in the filtration and distribution plants.

31

The destruction of the landscape, the forests, and the mountains didn't start with the construction of the dams. It started well before that, and is one of the irreversible consequences of the civil war. It is rare to see a conflict leading to an intense increase in building projects which, paradoxically, had more devastating effects than the destruction and ravages of the war itself. But that's what happened here, where paradoxes abound. During the civil war, total deregulation, anarchy, and the absence of any oversight in applying the laws led to wild urbanization, stimulated by population shifts, speculation, and conspicuous consumption caused by the influx of money from arms and drug sales controlled by the militias and by the intense development of unregulated commercial practices.

Far from being brought to a halt by the return of peace, the deregulation that led to breakneck urbanization and irremediable ecological destruction continued during the ghastly second republic, when all excesses were legalized, as long as they earned money, always money, more and more money. I described all these mechanisms in my novel *L'Empereur à pied*, which very few readers interpreted as also being about the destruction of the environment and the devastation of a country through the physical violence inflicted upon it. For thirty years, the construction of monstrous buildings disfigured the towns and mountainsides. Individuals and groups who had been close to the militias, and who had become developers and unscrupulous billionaires in the orbit of power during peacetime, grabbed whole stretches of the coastline and beaches, then built them up and privatized them arbitrarily. The same species of men gutted, smashed, and carved up whole mountains to extract the sand required for cement factories, and these quarries caused ghastly holes to appear in some of the country's most beautiful landscapes. In 2008–2009, an advertisement financed by environmentalists portrayed Lebanon as a beautiful young woman receiving repeated blows, injuries, splinters, wounds, until she is completely disfigured and a horrifying sight. The commercial was so disturbing it was banned. Denial was still strong, and no one wanted to see what was going on. And yet the disfigured face of the country was always there before our eyes, and the work of destruction was increasing every day. Mind-boggling contracts continued to be signed, and monstrosities continued to be built against the law. Laws closing the quarries enacted by force were flouted and the despoiled public beaches were never restored because they belonged de facto to members of the caste that held the government hostage.

32

The total impunity of this caste also allowed its principal leaders to endow themselves with the priceless gift of an off-book fund each, fed by government revenues but unanswerable to any auditing, any accounting requirements, or any documentation of expenditure. Berri awarded himself the fund for the development of the southern region, Jumblatt the one intended to finance the repatriation of people displaced by war, and Hariri the one for the reconstruction of Beirut. These funds allowed them to finance their political goals, to buy the loyalty of their factionalized clients, and to enrich their principal fiefs by encouraging embezzlement, fictitious projects, and padded invoices. The depth of the black hole they caused in public finances is still unknown today, as is their undoubtedly enormous contribution to the general downfall. At the same time, one government after another gave the pretext of all kinds of difficulties to avoid having to pay the relatively modest sums they owed by law to municipalities, social security, or organizations supporting disabled people. Of course it's true they weren't that profitable.

What were profitable, very profitable in fact, were the port and the customs service, through which thousands of tons of goods passed every day, as well as the airport, the motor vehicle registration service, and the Casino du Liban. At one time or another all these institutions also had their own off-book funds, whose accounts were never subject to any kind of scrutiny for over thirty years, and where more than twenty billion dollars are said to have disappeared.

33

I n thirty years, the entire country became the private hunting ground of the caste of oligarchs in power, which established a relationship with the citizenry similar to a mafia's, offering protection, guarantees, and small opportunities to all those who asked for them, and preventing any form of access to government officials except petitioning. This oligarchy created excessive factionalism in the state sector by confiscating all public services and their administrative apparatus, putting a stranglehold on all ministries, municipalities, and other public entities, then dividing up areas of responsibility along religious lines. All this resulted in, among other aberrations, the padding of the bureaucracy with tens of thousands of newly created fictitious jobs, which put a considerable strain on the public purse. To say nothing of the fact that entire pointless organizations continued to exist, and to be provided with directors and secretaries and orderlies to this day. The administration service for the railroads, for example, is still operating, although there has not been a single rail or a single train anywhere in the landscape for sixty years. A mysterious "office of the flag," no doubt intended to ensure that all representations of the national flag accord with the rules set out in the constitution, costs millions. And salaries are still being paid to public servants who have been dead for eons, along with lifelong indemnities to the descendants of all members of Parliament, unto the nth generation. It's all very banana republic, and it would almost be funny, Kafkaesque, or absurd, if it weren't coupled with the total indifference and arrogance of the oligarchy in power, which naturally never manages to agree on the government budget—not out of concern for the accuracy of the accounts, but because the shares of the cake are not considered equitable by one or another of its members.

This arrogance reached its apogee on January 22, 2019, during the Davos Forum, when a Lebanese minister, who was also the son-in-law of President Aoun, proudly declared that Lebanon could give lessons to the rest of the world on how to run a country, and could teach the great nations, such as Great Britain and the United States, how to govern without a budget.

34

July 18

Until the evening of October 17, 2019, we might still have believed that we would be living with all this for another hundred years. Of course there was the first civil uprising of 2015, during the trash crisis. But after that, for five years, only tiny groups of activists continued to protest, shouting themselves hoarse, bravely and pointlessly, until the fated evening of October 17. A week beforehand, there had been the wildfires and the scandal of the firefighting aircraft stuck on the ground because the money for their maintenance had evaporated. This had not provoked any street protests, only virtual indignation on social media. And then suddenly, on the evening of October 17, the government announced that calls on WhatsApp, a free platform, would be taxed. Another measure to camouflage, if only for a few weeks and in the most ridiculous way possible, the enormous fiscal hole and terrible impending bankruptcy of the entire state sector. The banks had already been dangerously teetering for two months. A minuscule tax, almost nothing, and the bucket, already filled to the brim, spills all over the place.

During the night of October 17, the ranks of protestors, who had been only a handful for years before then, swell considerably as they occupy the central squares of all the towns in the country. On the morning of October 18, all the main thoroughfares, the highways, the regional roads, and all the main city roads are blocked by burning tires and dumpsters. The schools and banks do not open and stay closed for weeks. In the afternoon of October 18, hundreds of thousands of protestors occupy Martyrs' Square and Ryad al Solh Square, in the center of Beirut. In the following days, more than a million demonstrators are counted in the various gathering places throughout the country. The roads stay closed for several days. Over the following weeks the movement grows, as do the protests, with one single demand: the end of the current political class, the resignation of the government and the appointment of a caretaker cabinet to manage the financial crisis. A few politicians, ex-parliamentarians or ministers, who declare themselves to be in opposition, are chased away whenever they try to join the protestors. On October 29, the Shiite militias and police auxiliary troops affiliated with the guard of the speaker of Parliament Nabih Berri attack the protestors. Saad Hariri's cabinet resigns a few hours later. From November onward, the demonstrations end in confrontations with the police and sometimes directly with members of Nabih Berri's Amal Movement. In the heart of the mountains, in the Bisri Valley where a dam was being planned, protestors are camped permanently to stop any progress on the project, and notably any uncontrolled deforestation. On December 15, the former prime minister Fouad Siniora is booed for forty-five minutes before the start of a concert at the assembly hall of the American University of Beirut and ends up being obliged to leave the venue. From that day onward, politicians and members of their entourages, who already assiduously kept a low profile, are systematically identified and chased away from public places, restaurants, and stores.

35

July 20

I called a repairman today because two of our air-conditioning units are having problems and are not cooling much anymore. He was a huge young man, with colossal strength, his face mask covering only a portion of his massive, fashionably trimmed beard. He groaned as he worked, I could easily imagine him carrying heavy beams around rather than fiddling with wires in narrow conduits and cleaning little filters with the ends of his chunky fingers. He was perched up on his ladder working away when Nayla came home from her practice and seemed surprised to find him there, as when you meet someone you know but not where you usually see them, which causes some confusion and a moment of doubt. He on the other hand didn't hesitate, he recognized her immediately and seemed quite happy to see her. My wife, having made sure that he was who she thought he was, asked how he was doing. He replied that he was out of work, and that he had gone back to his first job as an electrician. Usually I don't get involved with these kinds of sudden encounters because they can often be my wife's patients, so I wait to be brought into the conversation, or not. Nayla's practice doesn't necessarily demand distance or neutrality. But I found it difficult to imagine, I don't know why, that this big guy was one of her patients. In fact she asked him how his son was doing, and he replied: "Better, much better. They've lowered the dose on his medication." Then he added with a laugh, his huge torso dancing up and down, that he was the one who needed sedatives and anti-anxiety drugs now, just like everybody else.

When he had started fixing the air-conditioning units, the man had told me he used to be a valet parking attendant before the financial crisis, and added that it used to be a lucrative job. I knew that, I've always hated valet parking attendants in Beirut. Before the collapse those guys were a real mafia, colonizing the busy streets where the bars, pubs, and nightclubs were, instituting their own laws, commandeering all available parking spaces, and then charging outrageous rates for them. Or they would take your car and you had to wait a long time before it was brought back to you, and you would have no idea what they were up to with it while you were having dinner or out late with your friends. They have mostly disappeared now, and I must admit I'm not at all upset about it. But I didn't say this to my electrician, especially since his easygoing demeanor, his spontaneous cheerfulness, made me regret thinking ill of his colleagues. In any case, that's how I realized, at the end of his conversation with my wife, that he knew her from the time, not so long ago, when he was a valet parking attendant and we used to go to Abd El Wahab restaurant on the street where he worked. I couldn't remember him. But one day when Nayla went there by herself with some friends, he had found out she was a psychotherapist and asked her advice about his son, and she had referred him to a pediatric specialist. Every time he saw her and took care of her car, he would give her any news of his boy's treatment, and she would listen to him patiently for several minutes.

When he finished repairing the air conditioners and I asked him how much I owed him, he looked like a little boy caught being naughty by his teacher. He couldn't bring himself to name a figure; because of inflation it was such an enormous sum he was ashamed of it, and I found him incredibly endearing, despite his size, his beard, and his mask. I also guessed he was hesitant about asking for money out of consideration for my wife, who had helped him a lot, as he mumbled repeatedly. He seemed dazed in admiration before her. He's not the first. We were standing in front of the French doors leading onto the terrace. As I was insisting he tell me his price without any further ado and repeating that he wasn't responsible for inflation, a pigeon suddenly landed on the terrace railing, just a couple of steps away from us. We were silent for a few seconds as we looked at this unexpected striking apparition, this sudden crystallization of a quivering animal staring at us and tilting its tiny head, presenting us with one of its inexpressive round eyes. Every time this scene occurs, I think of the first page of *The Palace* by Claude Simon, and of the description of the magical transmutation of a pigeon on a windowsill, in Barcelona, in 1938, a description that it occurred to me right then was probably inspired by the magnificent scene of the appearance of the stag in the middle of the forest in Faulkner's *Go Down, Moses*, which I had recently read. My giant electrician pulled me away from these fleeting thoughts, declaring that we would soon be so hungry we would end up eating these kinds of animals. I was thinking about the stag. He was talking about the pigeon. I replied that it would be a while before that happened, that we were too proud for that.

36

On February 11, 2020, a new government was formed, against the will of the millions of citizens who had been protesting for four months. To make everyone believe that their voices had been heard, the cabinet was composed of unknown people, who were supposedly independent. It soon became clear that they were all close to the senior politicians and leaders of the incumbent parties, notably Hezbollah, the Amal Movement, and the movement of General Aoun and his son-in-law. The other parties declared themselves to be in opposition, even though when the day came to vote in Parliament, they gave their confidence to the party they claimed to reject. In any event, the only way you could possibly de-scribe that cabinet is as a puppet show. Since then, in other words for five months now, even as the economic crisis has only continued to escalate past points of no return, and as the collapse is complete in all sectors of the economy, nothing is being done, no resolutions, no decisions, no action plans, nothing.

37

July 21

For a few weeks now I've sensed that Nayla is exhausted when she comes home from her practice. Through her work she knows that the financial and public health crises and the lockdowns awaken fears and more long-standing problems in each of us that can be psychologically devastating when they are revived. She is starting to feel this herself. On top of all this, she keeps telling me that her patients' problems are echoing more and more with what she is experiencing herself when faced with the disintegration of everything around us, and she sometimes feels overwhelmed by emotion and complex, exhausting sensations. I noticed three or four days ago that she was regularly sitting down to her computer to write, and for longer spells than when she was just answering emails or preparing notes or short presentations. She finally admitted to me that she was doing a peculiar exercise, prompted by the pressing need to purge herself of all the violent feelings she was experiencing—a kind of self-therapy, for herself and with herself, which she writes down every day, creating a session where she is both the therapist and the patient, engaged in a conversation. She let me read the first sessions.

MY THERAPY WITH MYSELF

First Session

I'm feeling very nervous about starting this session, and even quite a high degree of anxiety. I actually have no idea what kind of a therapist I will turn out to be for myself, and especially how I, as a patient, will play this game. But it's clear that if I'm talking about a "game," then my resistance is already firmly in place. We'll see how this goes.

THERAPIST: *I'm listening.*
PATIENT: *For a while now, specifically since the end of lockdown, I've started feeling anxious, especially at the end of the day and when I'm going to bed, which is causing me huge sleep problems.*

TH: *Since the end of lockdown, you say? Was there a specific event that set off your anxiety?*

P: *Not really. But two things gradually became unbearable to me: social media and the Netflix series we were watching every night back then.*

TH: *What do you mean by unbearable? How were they unbearable?*

P: *Social media started to feel suffocating to me. Literally. After three or four minutes looking at my Instagram or Facebook accounts, my breath would become labored and I'd start to feel a heavy weight in my chest and an urge to shout, to run.*

TH: *Shout what? Run where?*

P: *I don't know.*

TH: *Are you noticing that your anxiety is rising now, as you're talking to me?*

P: *Yes.*

TH: *Where do you feel it?*

P: *It grabs me here, in my throat, it's suffocating me.*

TH: *And these tears?*

P: *Frustration, lots of frustration.*

TH: *Can you say a little more about that?*

P: *I can't stand reading all those endless cynical posts, talking about our failure, or ceaselessly repeating that we were helpless faced with the people in power. But I do feel that it's true that all our efforts during the revolution were actually in vain. No* one heard us. No one cared about our demands. It makes me want to scream, to howl...

TH: Anger and sadness resulting from a feeling of helplessness?

P: Absolutely.

TH: And this helplessness, is that something you have felt before, when you were young, because people wouldn't listen to you?

P: (A pause.) No one has ever listened to me. (Tears.)

TH: Yes, let your sadness come... Who never listened to you?

P: My mother and father, each in their own way.

TH: Who do you want to start with?

P: My mother. When she was cross with me, I remember she took on this cold and distant attitude, which lasted for days. She wouldn't even speak to me, as if I didn't exist anymore. It didn't matter that I cried in my room, noisily and sometimes for hours, hoping that she would end up relenting or taking pity on me and come and console me—all in vain. Nothing softened her: not my tears, nor my swollen eyes, nor my upset face, nor sighs, nor hunger strikes... I always had to go apologize to her in order for our relationship to gradually return to normal.

TH: And now, right here, what are you feeling? I see that you have changed posture, that you're sitting up straighter in your chair.

P: Yes, I'm angry at her.

TH: And if you were to express this anger in words, what would you say to your mother? "Maman, I'm angry at you because..."

P: ...

TH: "Maman, I'm angry at you because..."

P: ... I'm angry at you because when you were cross with me, when I was little, you abandoned me, you let me cry alone, in despair. You remained cold in the face of my distress and you were deaf to my suffering. I had to bend, to break myself, to bow my head and come apologize, every time, for you to deign to reinstate me in your field of vision and hearing, for me to exist for you again. I can remember several times during those humiliating apology exercises when you made a point of correcting me, explaining that it wasn't enough, in good French, to just say "I'm sorry," that I had to say, "I apologize, Maman!" That was all you cared about, my using the correct phrase, more than my distress.

TH: Keep talking to her: "That was all you cared about, whereas all I wanted was for you to—"

P: —All I wanted was for you to treat me as a mother would and not like an indifferent tormentor, for you to take me in your arms, for you to tell me that you loved me no matter what, that nothing was worth causing me such pain...

I interrupt the session. I'm allowed to do that, I'm just here with myself after all. I know what comes next, naturally... Don't bother, it's okay, I heard you, I understand. Our leaders' arrogant indifference to the country's collapse, to our demands, and to our hatred suffocates me and plunges me into a state of high anxiety because in fact it is my suffering in the face of my mother's indifference and deafness from long ago that is being reawakened in me... Except that I've also just understood that I am no longer the distressed little girl who has to suppress her anger in order to protect her relationship with her mother...

38

Second Session

Th: What brings you here today?
P: Over the same period that we've been talking about
since we began, in other words for about three
months now, I've been feeling very tired after my
sessions with my patients. It's as if their problems
are suddenly affecting me directly. I can no longer
find the right emotional distance between us. I
don't understand why I've become so vulnerable
when I've always been so proud of not letting other

*people's suffering overwhelm me, while also not
losing my empathy.*

*Th: Can you give me an example of a session that you
found particularly affecting?*

*P: Last week a new patient was telling me about how
he was endlessly mourning his mother. She died a
year ago from cancer. You know how much I like
working on grief with my patients and you also
know that, despite my own situation, this very
frequently recurring topic doesn't affect me on a
personal level. I've worked with patients at all
stages of illness, treatment, and remission, and
with other patients whose family members were
cancer sufferers or victims.*

Th: So what was different with this patient?

*P: When he was talking about his mother and her last
days, I felt anxiety, I had trouble breathing, and I
disconnected from him for a moment and suddenly
found myself imagining her death. That had never
happened to me before.*

Th: What did you imagine?

P: Her physical decline.

Th: Keep going.

*P: He was talking about his pain at seeing his mother,
who was once so beautiful and lively, turn into an
old woman who had everything wrong with her. It
was his sadness, his distress at seeing her physical*

decline that upset me, much more than the state his mother was in during her terminal phase.

Th: But then... Why this time, and not with other patients?

P: I know, I've done the work on myself, and I thought I had dealt with my fear of dying.

Th: But if I understand this correctly, your distress mostly comes from your identification with the observer, the witness to the illness, not with the sick woman herself.

P: Yes. With another patient, who had survived two bouts of cancer, it was the word "dignity" that had come between us. I'm not even sure who said the word first. What is terrible with this illness, and with the invasive treatments that people undergo in the hope of a so-called cure, is that it takes away a human being's dignity.

Th: Interminable mourning, physical decline, loss of dignity...

P:...

Th: Interminable mourning, physical decline, loss of dignity...

P:...

Th: Interminable mourning, physical decline, loss of dignity... You're crying. Yes, go ahead, that's good, cry...

P: It's not me I'm crying about.

Once again I interrupt the session. I know what I'm crying about, now, but mostly I know why that session with my patient was so difficult. That sick woman, with aggressive lung cancer, suffocating, calling for help, losing her vital organs one by one, losing her dignity and autonomy along with them, that woman is not me. I was not overcome by pity or the fear of death. It's not that the young man's story reminded me of the illness I carry inside me either. I've just understood that this son's mourning, the heartache he experiences again every day from having seen his mother perish, is another loss that I have been experiencing myself, for a few months now. A loss I didn't want to face, that I still find hard to admit to, but which is real and pressing and overwhelming. I'm finding it hard to say, to write... But it's about this country, which is in physical decline too, in its death throes in fact, it's about the loss of everything we did, the splendor of our former lives, everything we dreamed of, and all the other potential deaths to come...

39

July 22

There are many reasons why the government held on to power in the end, and didn't cave under pressure from the population and street demonstrations. There is the obstinate resistance of all those who were embroiled in thirty years of corruption and can sense that, if they don't hang on at any price and obstruct even the slightest change, they will be carried off with no mercy. There is the power of the traditional political parties and the alarms of factionalism that they know how to sound when it suits them. And among those parties is the most dangerous one of all, Hezbollah, the only party that is still armed, on the pretext of fighting the

Israeli occupation of the southern provinces where there have been no Israeli troops for fifteen years, but in fact so that the party can be used as an instrument of pressure and destabilization in Syrian and Iranian hands.

At the time of the October 2019 uprising, Hezbollah tried to show that it was in favor of governmental reform. Like other parties, in the first few days it authorized its members and supporters to join the protests. Then it became more hard-line, no doubt because things seemed to be getting out of control. It apparently couldn't allow itself to contemplate any changes in government because that would entail reevaluating its strategic choices and putting the Syrian-Iranian axis, of which it was an essential part, at risk. Shortly afterward the Shiite community was largely forced to renounce its demands for the end of the corrupt regime, an end it was hoping for just as much as other citizens were. Hezbollah also let its allies in the Amal party and sometimes even its own sympathizers provoke or confront the protestors. After a few months of hesitation and prevarication, the two Shiite parties and their allies in President Aoun's circle finally created a new puppet government on February 11, whose rallying cry appears to be mostly to do nothing at all, except continue the same practices with the same arrogance, such as the mafialike divvying up—not of the cake that doesn't exist anymore, but of the key posts in government agencies, just in case manna might fall from the sky again after all.

40

July 23

can't stop wondering, every time we go into a pub or a restaurant—there being no other forms of entertainment left anymore—how people can continue to eat and drink and pay the checks that are almost the same amounts as before the economic crisis. Marylin, the cheerful and always enthusiastic manager of Super Vega, explained one evening that she serves almost no meat anymore, because it is too expensive now, or avocados, for the same reason, when one of the most delicious items on her menu was based on them. And that everything else is from local producers, fresh fruit and vegetables, but also liquor, especially gin, and beer of course.

As for whiskey and tequila, she has to sell them at a loss or significantly raise the prices she charges.

A few months ago, Youssef Fares, who is an olive oil producer, explained to me that since the end of the war even the so-called local products are actually completely dependent on imports, because of the banks' absurd interest rate policies and the government's complete indifference to everything, and to business in particular, which mean that Lebanon is producing absolutely nothing anymore. Which also means, as he told me after a protest when we were in a café and all around us other protestors also taking a break were setting down flags and banners on the nearby seats, which also means that in his business for example, everything, absolutely everything, from the bottles to the corks to the labels, everything is imported. Our so-called local products are in fact largely made up of imported goods, and with the rise in the dollar, that local production is not much cheaper than the imports anymore.

I recalled this conversation and relayed it to Marylin, who declared that there are always ways to solve these kinds of problems. For example to get the excellent local gin, her restaurant buys a few bottles from the producers, who then agree to refill them when they are empty. "Just like demijohns back in the day," I said. "We're going back to the old trading models." Marylin laughed, or at least I think she did. I told her that if we met her in the street by chance, we wouldn't recognize her, because she always wears a face mask. She laughed again, you could see it in the sparkle in her eyes.

41

asked the same question of Adonis, the owner of Café de
Pénélope, which is actually a restaurant, not far from Badaro
Street, under the pine trees of the Kfoury district. When I was
giving an interview to a journalist from *Le Monde* a few years
ago, I had suggested we meet at Penelope's, as we used to call
it, and the restaurant's name had appeared in the prestigious
newspaper. Adonis was grateful for this, and ever since then
we always have a chat or a discussion when we go to his place
for a meal. His cuisine is sophisticated and his music excellent. There's also a screen with nonstop clips from Charlie
Chaplin or Buster Keaton silent films. I sometimes meet my

students here too, to talk about their progress on their theses or dissertations, and I've even gotten into the habit of calling the café "my office" or "my cafeteria." I told Adonis how one of my books, *Villa des femmes*, is a kind of rewriting of Homer's *Odyssey*, and that the villa in question is none other than Penelope's house. I've been thinking lately that, in this period of mass departures, in this unceasing Odyssean movement, with young people dreaming of emigration and old people forlornly fantasizing about returning to the land, Penelope is the symbol of anchorage, of resistance to thugs taking the country hostage, like the frightfully vulgar suitors besieging Odysseus's house and family in the Homeric epic.

I've never bored Adonis with these interpretations of the name of his establishment, although I'm sure he'd be keen to hear them. He's a handsome, athletic young man, a good fit with his namesake, even if my wife thinks that his beard and his black shoulder-length hair make him look more like the classical representations of Jesus Christ. To me, he does look a lot like a kind of Greek god or hero, just like his namesake in fact. The Adonis of legend is part of our national mythology, but he is also a symbol of resurrection, like Osiris, Dionysus, or the Christ. The ancient fable has him dying from being charged by a wild boar in the gorges of a torrent south of Byblos, now called Nahr Ibrahim—gorges of sublime beauty, which were obviously devastated by the recent construction of a dam—and being reborn every spring in the same place. I don't know what our Adonis thinks of the fact that his name is associated with the hope of rebirth. Good things, no doubt.

And yet last time we ate at his restaurant, when I asked him how he was getting on, he just shrugged. "Surviving," he added. "We just have to get through this." And then he had that look that we all have when we think about the new government's incredible powers of inertia and about their lack of any attempt whatsoever to find a solution to the disaster that is sweeping us all away. At the moment, for our Adonis, rebirth is not really the issue.

42

July 24

There have been Israeli planes roaming the skies for a few days now. You never see them, but their rasping groan suddenly rises, then lasts a few long minutes before fading into the distance and falling silent. Yesterday Hezbollah claimed an attack against Israeli soldiers. Everyone tends to believe that the Shiite party might provoke a war and complete the devastation of what is left of the country in order to save its own stake and that of the Syrian-Iranian axis. Only the rich can get loans. But nothing happens. I actually think Hezbollah knows that a conflict would sink it straight down to the ocean floor along with the rest of the ship. It's already taking on water on all sides, in Syria and Yemen, and its Iranian mentor is too, even more so. Its own local base is not in a position to cope with another war. And Israel for its part is happy to see it flounder. On that account at least, we have nothing to worry about for a while.

43

There are always people who love to dance among the ruins. And in a country where conspicuous consumption is seen as the most exciting lifestyle, of course it became a must to show off how little one was affected by the economic crisis. So there they all are, the indifferent rich, gathered together up there in the luxury chalets and nightclubs of a tony ski resort turned high-altitude spa for the occasion. Swimming pools, bars, dance parties, banquets, laughter, and joie de vivre. "We're supporting the economy, aren't we?" Not that they even feel the need to salve their consciences. And quite a few Lebanese designers and restaurant owners are compelled to have a stand or a table in the midst of it all too, because that's where the money is, lots of money, no doubt largely acquired from thirty years of corruption and siphoning public funds. People on social media are outraged, pictures of a kid playing with dollars as if they were a rattle go viral. And then suddenly the ghastly, invisible virus also makes an appearance at the party, and soon multiplies because no one there cares about social distancing, they are rich, they feel protected even from infection. In a single day, the clubs, the restaurants, and the pubs all empty out, the deafening music falls silent, the chalets are locked up in haste, the mountains are left in their primeval peace.

44

July 25

This morning Mariam told me there is a leak under the sink. After the washing machine, the air-conditioning units, the drinking water dispenser, and the pump that brings water into the building, here at last is something that has nothing to do with the unreliable electricity supply. I was almost happy about it. I was starting to feel harassed by the sense that we are permanent victims of a malevolent force that derails and wrecks everything, and there is nothing we can do about it. The plumber arrived. He is a funny guy with a deep voice, grumpy and talkative, always telling stories as he works about his prowess in plumbing, but in an original way, like an epic saga or a Netflix series. He always starts with a terrible problem that almost brings him to his knees, then he creates suspense by listing all the failed attempts to remedy it, before at last describing the solution he came up with, which is always spectacular. And with good reason. Today's tale is the one about the incredibly complex unblocking of a drain in a multistory building. He'd tried everything, it was still blocked, but he finally used kerosene, which he poured into the pipe and set alight. It exploded with the pressure, and then, he added, taking as his witness his apprentice who concurred with everything, the drain covers on every floor literally popped out, along with all the blockages, while the manhole cover in the street propelled a car parked above it into the air like a spring, and a guy ran out of the building with a mattress on his back, thinking it was an Israeli attack. I felt like he was telling me a gag from Gaston Lagaffe, and I didn't know quite what to believe, not that I know anything about plumbing, but I still thought it was far-fetched, despite his apprentice's confirmation.

The apprentice was nothing like the type you would expect: he was an old man, a little tired, bent and anxious, constantly jiggling his knee. The plumber spoke to him deferentially and only asked him to do small favors. In the end, he asked him very politely, almost apologetically, to go down to the car to get a box of joints. When the old worker left, the plumber took the opportunity to tell me that the poor guy was his brother, fifteen years his senior. He had been working in a furniture factory that laid him off, giving him three months' salary, but at the old rate, which meant he was left with nothing. "He came over to my place and begged me to give him something to do. But what can I give him to do? Nothing. He knows nothing of the trade. But I can't allow him to realize that. He's my older brother, he basically raised me and my brothers. So I bring him along with me, and that way he feels like he's working."

"What about welfare payments after he was laid off?" I asked. The plumber then reminded me that unemployment benefits are paid by the social security fund, which is bankrupt. I was ashamed to have asked such a ridiculous question.

"Not a single employee is going to see a shadow of their savings or contributions for years," he concluded. "The worst misery is yet to come. We haven't seen anything yet."

45

July 27

For over two years now, all international financial aid has been blocked, and one government after another has been warned it will be unblocked only if reforms are carried out at the highest level of the state sector, to stop corruption and make government spending more transparent. Nothing was done, naturally, for two years. The aid therefore never arrived, and the country collapsed. One of the reforms that was required, as Nadine, who works at the World Bank, often explained to me, is the computerization of the government accounts, which would allow all expenditure to be traceable. But of course that would terribly complicate the work of the whole gigantic apparatus of siphoned funds on which the political regime is built. The new cabinet, which promised to start the reform process, has done nothing, of course.

This evening a short demonstration in the city center of Beirut led to the closure of several main roads. At the end of the evening, I went to pick up Nadim at the home of one of his friends. I had to make several detours, the streets were blocked off, but there was no one about, only the ghostly dumpsters, burning through the night.

46

July 28

C ase numbers are rising again, and a temporary lockdown
is announced. For countless small retail businesses and
restaurants, this is the predicted culmination of the disaster.

Covid-19, the economic crisis, the bankruptcy of the
government, the stifling heat coming unusually early this
year, along with the electricity cuts and the distressing noise
like lawn mowers of Israeli drones overhead, the Damocles'
sword of war permanently hanging over us: what more does
it take to let loose a wave of cynicism on social media? Tri-
ple and quadruple punishment, the ten plagues of Egypt, a
whole lexicon playing on victimization, powerlessness, and

subjugation to predictable calamities that are said to have inescapably befallen us. A stupid custom of local TV stations is to host so-called soothsayers, who are very seriously accorded the status of oracles and whose pronouncements and predictions are endlessly analyzed and compared to current events to check how they match up. It's total desperation.

47

July 29

called the owner of the land in the mountains to discuss the price he is asking and the payment conditions again. He obstinately refuses to lower his figure and tries everything he can to get as much cash as possible. He can't seem to grasp the fact that I have no cash, that all we own is locked up in the bank and that I am prepared to give him almost the whole amount, that it will be transferred from my account to his. In the end he offers to sell me a smaller plot. I tell him I'll come have a look. I realized when I hung up the phone that my stubborn desire to own some land on which I can grow a few trees and especially build a little house, even if I don't quite know what with, is no longer just an old fantasy of someone from a traditionally urban family, but a kind of unconscious challenge. Buying a piece of land with the last pennies you have, dreaming of building something on it, those become acts of resistance to the very idea of collapse.

48

August 1

We celebrated Christmas last year with no decorations and no lights, in an extremely depressing gloom—this Christmas, which is in a few months' time, we might not even have a tree. Today, eight months later, we are celebrating the Feast of the Sacrifice with no sacrifices, since there are no more sheep. Bitter comments are spreading on social media: the sheep can sleep soundly this year, it's the people who are being sacrificed instead—a strange Christian interpretation of the idea of the substitution of the lamb.

I noticed some graffiti on a wall a few days ago with this fine inversion: *The government is trying to overthrow the people.*

49

August 3

Today's medley of bad news is endless, like every other day's: an announcement that ninety employees of the Mechanical Inspection Center are being laid off, and the salaries of all the others are being halved; a strike in the city council of Baalbek because salaries have not been paid; a new garbage crisis looming; a demonstration in front of the Ministry of Energy; violence and confrontations with the police.

On video footage shared by activists, you can hear, as we often have these last few months, a protestor shouting at the immobile, impassible police officers standing in front of him blocking his way. He is pointlessly haranguing them: "Who are you defending here? Who are you defending? Which government, which power?" Then he addresses one of them in particular, pointing at him: "You for example, how much do you make per month? A million and a half pounds, two million tops? And how much are your two million worth these days? What can you buy with that amount?" None of the officers reacts, they all look absent above their face masks, until one of them makes eye contact with the shouting protestor. He holds his gaze for a moment, it looks like a challenge, but then he finally lowers his eyes, then his head.

During the protests in October and November, as they faced the huge crowd, the singing, the slogans, the enthusiasm, some military personnel had lost their cool and burst into tears. They've hardened up since then.

50

August 4

Two months ago Sabine made the difficult decision to leave for Canada with her family. Like many others, she fears she will not be able to cope with the general deterioration in working and living conditions here. The bankrupt government, which is no longer subsidizing organizations that help special-needs people like her son, and the closure of the institution where he was being cared for were what made her decide to weigh anchor for good. It's particularly heartbreaking for her, because like so many others she had already emigrated from Lebanon with her parents, exactly thirty years ago, in 1990, following the calamitous wars of

General Aoun. And two weeks ago, when she set the date for her departure, now confirmed for August 7—another departure, reocurring like a curse under the presidency of the same General Aoun—she realized that the first time, thirty years ago, she had also left on August 7.

As the days go by, we follow the progress of her preparations with each of our visits to her: the house with nothing left in it, the belongings sold, the emptied-out living room, then the bedrooms, the walls, the floors. And suitcases replacing the furniture.

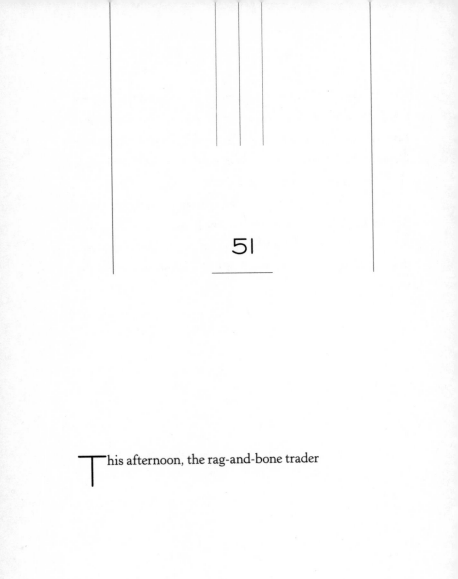

51

This afternoon, the rag-and-bone trader

52

August 10

I haven't been able to reopen this document until this morning. And today, as I do so, and reread the chapter I had just finished, and then the notes for the next one that I had jotted down before standing up just as the explosion occurred, I feel like I am reading stories from another era altogether.

As I read back into the fragments written over the past month, it's as if I were entering a room where a few distant memories of a happy time are preserved intact.

Which just goes to show...

53

As if that entire collapse I was describing was not happening fast enough, as if this degeneration was not swift enough, some unknown malignant force decided to precipitate them and in a matter of seconds hurled everything that was still standing to the ground.

54

Tuesday, August 4, 6:07 p.m. I'm working on the terrace where I've completed the chapter on Sabine's preparations for departure. Before going on with the next one, of which I've written the first few words, I stand up to take a plate of fruit I've just finished back to the kitchen, when I get a voice message. I set the plate down on the little table, open the message, and start listening to it, standing up. Suddenly the floor begins to move with incredible violence, accompanied by a sort of hideous roar. I'm petrified as I feel the terrace come and go beneath me like an old swing, and I think it's obviously an earthquake. My mind freezes, I'm standing stock still in the midst of the quake as if the least movement might increase my sense of total loss of control over everything, I don't do anything except repeat to myself: *it'll be over soon, it'll be over soon*, and I also think: *the children, the children*, or *the concrete is solid, it'll hold, the concrete is solid, it'll hold*, as my eyes see, without processing this information, how objects are falling all around me and smashing to the ground. And then everything suddenly stops moving and roaring, and I'm about to rush inside, but at that moment I'm nailed to the spot again, submerged by the deafening, interminable blast of a monstrous explosion, and this time my eyes seek out the familiar landscape around me, the trees, the buildings in the distance, everything that is always there before me and which now seems to be thunderstruck by the ghastly soundtrack flattening it. When this horror is over at last, I finally run inside while realizing that I still don't know what has happened, *an earthquake, sure, but then why that explosion?* or *an explosion, okay, but why an earthquake just before it?* But there are more urgent things to worry about: my panicked children, Nadim who has blood on his legs, and my wife who has gathered them up and is holding them together in her arms like a rampart against who knows what.

After a few more minutes of chaos, of fevered gesticulation—find something to wipe away the blood from Nadim's very light wound, go get some money and our identity cards, without stepping on the broken window glass, in case we have to leave and not come back if there's an aftershock—the first fragments of information start reaching us, in texts or phone calls, because cell-phone communication has not been cut off, and the unthinkable becomes clear: everyone we manage to contact, everyone who is already posting on social media or calling for help, everyone in the city seems to have experienced the same long nightmarish seconds, and that's what is so incomprehensible, because each of us thought at the time that it was just our house, our neighborhood, our street that was targeted, and we realize that we all were, at the same time.

55

The devastation from the explosion reached almost every part of the capital to varying degrees. But the most affected areas are undoubtedly the northern slope of the hill in Achrafieh and the city's entire northern seaboard, all the way from the central district to Ain el Mreisseh. And the most terrible destruction within all those areas occurred in and around the Gemmayzeh and Mar Mikhaël neighborhoods, from the port to the city limits of Bourj Hammoud. In a few seconds the blast destroys tens of thousands of apartments in the low-rise buildings and hypermodern skyscrapers scattered across this open stretch of land, blowing apart, pulverizing windows, glass, doors, furniture, and the inhabitants as well. But concrete is strong, the structures of the buildings hold, while hundreds of heritage residences are disemboweled and their old sandstone walls collapse on top of their occupants, while in a single second hundreds of cafés, restaurants, pubs, and stores are reduced to ruins, while scores of cars from the traffic on the avenue along the waterfront are hurled into the air, projected upward, then fall down again like toys, and thousands more in hundreds of streets are suddenly buried under thousands of tons of glass, tiles, and stones that cover the streets in an instant. And during those same few seconds the shock wave sweeps all the way up the hill of Achrafieh right to the top, then down the first few streets on its southern slope, laying waste in the blink of an eye to all the buildings, wards, operating rooms, and the whole population of the Saint George, Geitauoi, and Rosary Hospitals, and all the rooms and collections of the Sursock Museum, all the boutiques and their hundreds of shoppers and browsers in the ABC shopping mall, all the supermarkets, the smaller stores, the market stalls, the street vendors. And during those same few seconds, the same inexplicable and monstrous tempest blasts everything away in Bourj Hammoud, along the freeway toward Dora, through the Karantina district and its hospital in the east, and toward the hill of Ain el Mreisseh in the west, passing through Ghandak el Ghamik and the city center, where in a single instant virtually all the stores cease to exist. After that, for the next two or three minutes, the streets everywhere are filled with a white haze from all the dust and smoking debris, and the haggard pedestrians and residents who manage to get out are nothing but a fright of bloodied ghosts, while tens of thousands of men and women, who were living their lives in houses, offices, and businesses over an area the size of a whole city in itself, are now still prisoners in the rubble, the ruins, the blood, the cries, the calls for help . . .

56

During that evening of August 4, I had to take Nadine to the hospital. She was injured, she had told us so over the phone in the first minutes. She was at home with Camille when the first explosion happened (which we hadn't perceived on our side of the city, because it must have blended into the same thundering roar as the second one). They had jumped up just as the second and more destructive one detonated and its blast pulverized all the furniture and shot the pieces all around them. When they recovered their senses, they went outside to try to go to the emergency room at Rezek Hospital, walking through the rubble, the dust, the broken glass, and no doubt also the wounded and first responders and traffic jams of honking cars filled with the injured. But the emergency room was already at capacity. A pharmacist dressed her wound, but hours later she was still not well. I went to pick her up from her place, to try to get her to the Hôtel Dieu hospital, even though we knew that the chaos there had gotten even worse. The lack of electricity made the spectacle in the streets completely nightmarish. We had the sense that we were driving through a city that had been bombed for hours and hours. The headlights from the cars that were crawling along and the few places that were still lit up gave the visible destruction a phantasmagorical appearance. The noise of broken glass under our tires was constant, and the sidewalks looked like they were covered with the first fall of snow in some northern city. The traffic jams to get to the hospital were endless because some of the thoroughfares were blocked by ruins and collapsed buildings, and the emergency services and ambulances were howling without ceasing.

It was clearly impossible to get to the emergency room, and we had to content ourselves with some brief treatment outside the hospital walls, in the midst of immeasurable chaos and hundreds of casualties who were being attended to by the overwhelmed medical staff while lying on the ground or at the edge of garden beds covered in blood.

When I got home, I found one of my children's friends there. His parents had dropped him off at our place, after he had gone to his aunt's place and seen how she was injured and her house in ruins. He is the sweetest and gentlest boy, and he was trying to hide his anxiety and agitation that evening, but he couldn't keep still or stay seated for more than ten seconds at a stretch.

57

Since the evening of August 4, this: Reina is in intensive care, critically injured, Jad has a few superficial wounds, but no longer has a house, Omar is injured, Karim had left the office before the explosion happened, and so had his employees, which is just as well because there is no office anymore, Paula is unhurt because she went into the party headquarters' kitchen at the moment of the explosion, but Salam, who was in the large hall, has a head wound, Monique has an injured leg, she was attended to hastily at the hospital entrance because there were more urgent cases, a dentist friend put stitches into Nathalie's back without anesthetic, Paula and

Marwan's venerable publishing house is destroyed, Karine's house is blown to smithereens, Sandra's house is in ruins, so is Pierre and Nada's, Jean-Marc is dead, Michel's hotel is destroyed, Hatem's offices are smashed to pieces, Walid stitched up and dressed his brother's and nephew's wounds at home in the middle of the wreckage, Ralph's boutiques are nothing but heaps of rubble, Sophie's house is shattered, so is her mother's, Kamal's restaurant is a wreck, Rabih is injured and his workshop no longer exists, Michka is in the hospital in critical condition, but she'll pull through and so will her husband, the Moussas are safe but someone at their place was hurt and just a few seconds would have turned it into a tragedy, Marianna's house is badly damaged, Chantal was injured in her house and her mother died at her side, two people died in the Haifa building, the one where Marwan has his studio could collapse at any moment, Malak no longer has a house, there is nothing left of Rosa-Maria's store, Raïfé's house is in ruins, Marylin's mother is injured, the Coptis are miraculously safe, they were found under the rubble of their beautiful old home which almost completely collapsed on top of them and they were presumed dead, Tanit's gallery no longer exists, nor do Sarah's workshops, Tia is lightly injured but her house is destroyed, Bertrand's house is a ruin, he survived only by a miracle, and his children the same, but little Alexandra died

58

And also this: he was lifted up and thrown against the TV, *the couch flew up into the air and fell on top of her*, I walked through the streets like a sleepwalker before I realized that everyone around me was injured, *she was sitting on the stairs covered in blood, but I had no idea what to do to help her,* they ended up side by side on the ground, but neither of them could get up, *we lost track of her and finally found her at the Bhannes medical center,* the waiters rushed in shouting, then everything collapsed on top of us, *I heard her moaning but I was pinned under the windowpane,* she was hanging up the laundry and she rushed inside but then a piece of aluminum then an air-conditioning unit fell on top of her from the upper floor, *all the furniture in the room was sucked toward the back and a table flew up and smashed into his chest*, she went out of the store barefoot in the debris and the shards of glass, her shoulder broken and her hand in shreds, and a motorcyclist took her to the hospital on the back of his bike, *a piece of a window collapsed and broke his shoulder and tore off his ear*, she had to be taken out like a puppet through the broken car window, *when I got up again, his face was covered in blood and he was shouting and gesticulating at the wrecked house*, they stitched up her wound standing up in the hospital corridor, *it was chaos, my lab coat was covered in blood but I didn't know where I was hurt, I could hear screaming but I didn't know if it was the patients or the nurses and as I tried to get up I saw that the machines had crushed the patient on his bed*, she realized that her mother was killed instantly she couldn't do anything for her anymore, she went out into the street with a huge wound in her arm, *a car stopped and picked me up there were already three other injured people inside and blood everywhere, I never found out who the driver was*, she was found curled up in her armchair, she thought she was dead, *we barely had time to react to the first explosion when suddenly everything collapsed around us and I was lying underneath part of the counter with a terrible pain in my stomach*, they found it almost impossible to lift up the iron gate that had crushed him, *the dust was suffocating, I couldn't breathe anymore or see anything all I could hear was the screams*, she was thrown into the rubble and when she landed she had no injuries but she was dead, *I wanted to go back and get my glasses after the first explosion they were on the table I could see them there within reach but I couldn't move toward them and I realized I was injured in the leg and three seconds later there were no glasses and no table anymore and if I had been able to reach them I would have died*, he finally managed to get out from under the shelving that had collapsed on top of him but he couldn't stand up so he crawled to the doorway of his store, *she is so thin the blast broke one of her ribs*, it was chaos in the emergency room there was blood everywhere shouting crying people on the floor, on the countertops I was dressing the wound of a little boy lying on a desk when I raised my head and recognized my mother in the crowd completely covered in blood, *I found myself on all fours I had blood and white dust on my hands and my nose was bleeding*, the table was hurled against her and tore off her arm, *they tried to open the car door but they realized he was already dead*, he said he saw the bookcase fly into the air with all its contents and after that he heard her scream, *when I stood up again there was blood on the walls and bits of furniture, I didn't find them straightaway and I started calling for them screaming their names before I saw them coming toward me in the white darkness with blood on their legs*, his lungs burst, *everything collapsed there was nothing left*, they found him dead two hours later, *maybe she'll make it*, I don't know what happened to my cats

59

n five seconds: two hundred dead, one hundred and fifty missing, six thousand injured, nine thousand buildings damaged, two hundred thousand homes destroyed, as well as hundreds of historic or heritage buildings and four hospitals, ten thousand retail stores, workshops, stalls, boutiques, restaurants, cafés, pubs all reduced to rubble, scores of art galleries and studios belonging to painters, sculptors, stylists, designers, architects all swept away. In five seconds.

In September 2013, the MV *Rhosus*, a cargo ship registered under the Moldovan flag, sailing from Batumi and transporting 2,750 tons of ammonium nitrate destined for

Mozambique, makes a stopover, for reasons that no one has yet been able to ascertain, at the port of Beirut, where it is deemed unseaworthy and unable to continue on its voyage. The owner of the ship, a Russian by the name of Igor Grechushkin, refuses to pay the port fees, the cost of the necessary repairs, and the crew's salaries, and abandons the vessel to its fate. The owner of the cargo, a Georgian company called Rustavi Azot, renounces its claim to possession of the goods. In March 2014, this cargo is finally off-loaded at the port and stocked in Hangar number 12. A few months later, the ship sinks at the dock and the cargo is no longer claimed by anyone. Nobody cares, or only vaguely, and memos, but only memos, are sent by various offices to their overseeing ministries, without ever being taken any further. Some of these memos do reach the highest levels of the government, which accords them no attention whatsoever, and the cataclysmic cargo continues sleeping there for six years in the most perfect indifference. Except that experts in industrial chemistry consider it unlikely that the explosion was caused by the declared quantity. They think that the damage would have been much greater than it was. And yet that figure of 2,750 tons does appear on the manifest registered by the port authorities in September 2013. A portion of the ammonium nitrate might have been taken away and used in between times, which would mean that the cargo was not forgotten, was not sleeping, but was actually being used by a party whose identity remains a mystery, and used thanks to the complicity, corruption, collusion, political calculations, or strategies of a countless number of people.

Now of course all the aberrations regarding the history of this terrifying stock suddenly make sense. The lies no longer appear to be intended to cover up negligence or amateurism, but rather to hide more disturbing truths. An owner who abandons his ship, a ship that sinks in port, a company that no longer claims its cargo that is probably worth a fortune, a destination country that declares as naturally as you please that it has ordered a new supply because the first one simply never arrived, without worrying about the reasons why: everything points to this being a B-grade novel and leads us to believe that Lebanon was in fact the final destination. And especially that the stocked raw material was very probably being used, and from the very first day. The control that Hezbollah wields over the port inexorably leads to the conclusion that this use was being made under its aegis, and obviously for military purposes. Which would explain the silence of the port authorities, who would have turned a blind eye out of fear, collusion, or corruption.

As for finding out what directly caused the catastrophe, the hypotheses are numerous: an accident, an attack, airborne or not, or sabotage. The only certainty is that there was something burning for fifty minutes in a warehouse next to Hangar number 12. Everyone saw it, I followed the progress of the fire myself with relative indifference, not knowing what it would lead to, thanks to video clips shared on a WhatsApp group chat. What caused the fire remains a mystery, as do the contents of that neighboring warehouse. On the videos, at one point you can clearly distinguish strange streaks of light and crackling sounds, which led some port officials to claim that there was a stock of fireworks stored next to the ammonium nitrate. Those shameless lies and pantomimes only gave further credit to the hypotheses that the burning neighboring warehouse in fact contained weapons or munitions, which would make the contents of the two hangars absurdly homogeneous and consistent.

Whether the fire was accidental or whether it was arson, whether there were weapons nearby or not, all those distinctions no longer matter anymore. Whatever the case, whether it was one or the other or something else altogether, whatever the circumstances that led to this situation in the port of Beirut, the result is one and the same: on August 4, 2020, at 6:07 p.m., the cargo—or whatever was left of it, whether it was heated by the nearby fire or blown up by a nearby explosion in a weapons store or bombed from the air—exploded. Six years of lack of transparency and accountability, the result of thirty years of corruption and lies, of mafialike practices, of collusion between the various arms of government, the various ministries, political parties, and their clients, of devious geopolitical scheming and sinister warmongering by bloodthirsty, criminal militias, all this was concentrated, condensed in the most terrifying manner, and generated that five-second apocalypse.

60

August 11

Ever since the first night, our children have had spells of deep depression. They're having trouble making sense of what has happened to us. The solution they found in the end was to go out on the ground, to join the thousands of people—young people in particular—who have started on the work of cleaning up, of clearing away the rubble, in the absence of any involvement or assistance from government agencies, which have all completely disintegrated, or from the cabinet, which is nothing but a farce. We helped them get in touch with volunteer organizations, most of which are overstaffed and don't need any more workers. Never, since the beginning of the uprising last October, had such a spontaneous movement pushed so many people out into the streets, and never had the devastated streets been so full, invaded by a tide of people carrying brooms, shovels, masks, helmets, offering food and drink as if they were in a rage to do something, to refuse to allow themselves to be beaten, in a kind of festival of despair. They worked amidst the ruins of collapsed houses and wrecked small buildings, in the shadow of the huge destroyed skyscrapers, vanquished monsters that are still standing, disturbing and fascinating at the same time, like fearsome ghosts but also the proof that we are not on our knees.

In the end, Saria, Nadim, and their friends were asked to go to the Saint George Hospital, where the damage is enormous. But when they got there, there were already so many volunteers that they were not able to help. They were then sent to an apartment where they were needed and put in charge of sweeping away the rubble and sorting out what could be saved, with the help of the family of the old couple that lived there. The two old people had been injured. There was blood on the floor and in the debris.

61

They were also called on to clear out a doctor's office. When they came home, they had photos of objects that made them laugh: a Bakelite telephone, an old cassette and record player unit, both items of complicated machinery in their eyes, which reminded them of the cockpits of spacecraft in outdated science fiction movies. They didn't always understand what these objects were for, and I wondered what they were all doing in a modern-day doctor's office. Saria told me that it was actually the office of an old physician, who had died a long time ago, but whose children had kept it in its original state ever since. She showed me a picture of a fifty-pound note, out of circulation since the 1980s, which she had found in a drawer that had been thrown out of its compartment by the explosion. I imagined that this was the last fee the doctor received, which had stayed in a drawer for fifty years.

That doctor's office preserved from the world's forward march for fifty years obviously made me think of Iver Grove, the house described by W. G. Sebald in *Austerlitz*. But unlike what happens at Iver Grove, where the present makes cautious contact with what had stayed suspended for forty years, here time had been kept at a distance, and now brutally rushed in. It did so with the same violence in many other parts of the city, where the past was held differently, compressed and almost embalmed with the miserly jealousy of aristocratic family traditions and genealogies. In many of the historic homes in Beirut's ravaged neighborhoods, the ancient furniture and decor are now nothing but dust, ruins, and debris. The slow, meticulous sedimentation of time was swept away in a few seconds by the blast of a vengeful and incomprehensibly cruel present.

62

There are countless videos of the few seconds that preceded the explosion, then of those that followed it. Often the phones that were filming the warehouse fire jumped out of the hands that were holding them at the moment of detonation and after that there is nothing but a horrible mishmash of images. However, on recordings from public and commercial surveillance cameras, you can see a live stream, from above and in a kind of panoptical view, of the assassination of the city. The most difficult to watch are those from the hospitals, where you can see simultaneously and in a few seconds how the walls and ceilings in the patients' rooms, the hallways, the operating theaters, and the nurseries all collapse and crumble onto all the equipment, the furnishings, the machines, onto the patients, the medical staff, the visitors, and the newborn babies in their cribs.

63

The terrifying stories and eyewitness accounts of the thousands of casualties, of survivors, and of all those people struck by the sinister blast—we hear them and will continue to hear them for a long time to come. But we will never hear from the few dozen men and women who were at the port that Tuesday at 6:07 p.m., in front of Hangars 11 and 12, or at the foot of the grain silos. Those key witnesses of what happened at the very heart of the catastrophe are permanently silenced. There is nothing left of them except scraps of their last moments before they unknowingly entered what would be the last circle of hell. The firefighters and the young women paramedics called to the blaze, who can be seen in old photographs standing together in their uniforms, looking like science fiction heroes in astronauts' suits; the Syrian or Lebanese dockworkers who had stayed on after their regular shifts to do a couple of hours of overtime to earn three more dollars; the foreign workers, from Pakistan or Bangladesh: we celebrate them as heroes but their deaths are not accompanied by any stories. No one will ever be able to describe the astonishing violence with which lives—and the very materiality of bodies—can be erased at the precise place where 2,750 tons of explosive material explode.

64

August 12

For the last few days, the mornings have been especially difficult, from the moment I open my eyes and remember the immeasurable waste—of the city, the lost lives, and our futures. Nayla told me that she had woken up last night in the middle of the night wondering why she had a heavy weight on her chest, and wondering what had changed that she could no longer remember, and what more could have been added to the destruction of half the city, the economic crisis, and Covid-19. She had gone back to sleep in hope of not remembering it. In the morning she was relieved to hear that there was nothing more, nothing new.

During the day, my morale improves a little, notably at the sight of all those young people who rose like a single man to take on the task of erasing the signs of the nightmare and to help rebuild, given the inaction of the criminal government, whose members, even the most anonymous ones, are loathed and chased away as soon as they dare appear on the ground among the ruins. Also at the sight of the mobilization of civil society supported by an enormous international effort, and the solidarity of the entire population working together, having decided not to bend—or if the violence of the blows they received forced them to bend, not to break.

65

The Gemmayzeh and Mar Mikhaël districts, those most damaged by the explosions, were inhabited for over a century by the merchant aristocracy up in the hillsides and by a migrant population from the mountains and Armenian refugees on the plain below. Up until the beginning of the 2000s, Gemmayzeh and Mar Mikhaël were made up of little streets lined with artisanal and mechanical workshops, and all kinds of retail businesses. In the first years of the twenty-first century, in keeping with a worldwide trend, this neighborhood was transformed by the arrival of architects' offices, stylists' and painters' studios, and art galleries that were some of the most important in the Middle East. Among the preserved traditional heritage buildings, large-scale architectural projects were developed that showcased Lebanon's contemporary creativity. This activity then spread to the industrial wastelands and warehouse districts around the port, which were also taken over by Lebanese designers, artists, and galleries. The two districts all at once became centers of the nocturnal life that was emblematic of all the creative energy of Beirut.

This is what was irremediably destroyed by the explosion of August 4: the creativity and vitality of a people incarnated in its artists and designers, and their tireless, sometimes desperate desire to continue to exist, to ensure that their country exists through art, beauty, intelligence, and with a spirit that was all their own. They'd had to fight hard for that, as we all did, against the negative and morbid rationale of political power, its lethal corruption, and its arrogant ignorance. Only to see all their efforts, and those of so many others in all ways of life, flattened in a few seconds.

66

August 13

Today for the first time I have settled back down in the place where I usually work, here on the terrace, exactly where I was sitting a few seconds before the explosion, nine days ago, when I had just finished what has become chapter 50 of this book and jotted down the first few words of the next chapter. I had not come back to this table when I started writing again, not because of any kind of superstition, but because it has been very hot. Except that today, I need to tie up the broken thread of time again.

Nayla told me that she, on the contrary, was not going to start the account of her self-therapy again. There are other imperatives. She makes all her time available for urgent con-sultations, on top of her existing patients with whom she is now working on this recent trauma. The new requests are so numerous that she is overwhelmed with work, and she tells me that what she hears all day long is terrible. The hopeless-ness and exhaustion are boundless, but so is the anger.

67

On August 8, an absolutely massive crowd fills the vast expanse of Martyrs' Square and its surrounding streets again. Two hours before the appointed time, hundreds of thousands of protestors are already on-site to express their hatred for the whole political class. Very soon as well, the security forces, with dubious reinforcements under the authority of the speaker of Parliament, start to sow disorder by throwing tear gas grenades and shooting rubber bullets. It becomes more and more difficult to work out what the police are trying to protect from the crowd. They are blocking the protestors' access to the front of the ruined offices of the

An Nahar daily newspaper and to the carcass of the Le Gray Hotel. The city center they are blocking off is completely in ruins, there's not a single store or office left standing, the Parliament itself is ripped to shreds. And the whole government that it represents is nothing more than a broken cadaver.

On August 10, the government falls. This is the second one to collapse under the blows of protest and insurrection, without significantly affecting the mafia establishment that installed it, then let it go.

During the protest, one of my wife's former patients threw herself into her arms. She is a young activist, highly committed to the fight against the ruling class. Nayla told me she had come back from Britain to open up a patisserie shop and a line of fine food products, but the economic crisis had hit her hard and she had often thought about going abroad again. Then the explosion destroyed her premises. After we left, she no doubt stayed late on the front lines with the more pugnacious protestors, facing off against the security forces and the thugs that support them. Perched on a friend's shoulders, in the midst of the tear gas, the bullets, the flames, with a mask on her face and a scarf over her eyes, as she told Nayla the next day, she was shouting at the police officers covered in body armor like Michelin men: "We will not leave this country, we will stay here, we will be happy here again, we will laugh again, and if the bastards that you are protecting do not stand down, then we will go drink and dance on their graves."

68

August 14

ooking at the thousands of photos taken at the port and
posted on social media and news agency Web sites, I
realized how the colossal grain silos had been an emblem of
Beirut for me ever since I was a child and without my even
acknowledging it—much more so than the Pigeon Rocks or
Martyrs' Square—but also an emblem of Lebanon as a whole
in my eyes, almost more so than the columns of the Tem-
ple of Jupiter at Baalbek. I had started taking an interest in
that strange dinosaur when I was just a kid, after reading a
series in a *Tintin* magazine—which I have just astonishingly
remembered was called *The Petrified City* and was set in a

town that was struck by an incomprehensible attack which only the visitors to a silo survived. Later in life, I had used the fascinating grain silos at the port as the setting of a story that I never published or even finished. Hangar number 12 was at the foot of these silos. On August 4, their powerful concrete mass stopped the explosion from radiating farther west and destroying the rest of Beirut even more violently. In shielding the explosion with their enormous compact mass, they partially collapsed, and their sides crumbled down, disemboweled. But the remains, partly destroyed, are still standing, like a wounded beast or a cliff face eroded by ten thousand years of wind and waves, in the middle of the docks.

69

August 16

We walked over to the olive trees again, he and I, and then to the mulberry trees. This was another plot of land, the dry grass came up to our knees. Nayla and the children stayed at the boundary line, afraid of meeting some reptile or other. The heat was strong, despite a breeze that flowed through the dry wheat and made it rattle like an old wooden noisemaker. When we reached the ancient mulberry tree with its trunk twisted like hands begging for forgiveness, I stopped. I told the fellow that, with all the grass and despite his explanations, I couldn't make out the topography of the plot. He was beginning to annoy me. I told him his prices were too high for me, and he started up again with his grocer's prattle about high prices, cash, square meters. Nayla finally joined us, with Saria. Then at last Nadim decided to throw himself into the high grass as if he were diving into water. For a few days now, our children haven't stopped asking us to get out of Beirut. Saria in particular feels suffocated and incomprehensibly sad. Both of them feel very out of place whenever they are in the countryside, and no matter how hard I try to initiate them into its ways by telling them stories of my childhood days in the wilds of the high mountains, they always stay impervious to it all. But today, they seem happy, as if the idea of being able to escape the city was reassuring to them. They have been confronted, for the first time and in quite an abrupt manner, with the violence of history. They only knew about it through our old stories, but then it brutally appeared in their own familiar universe, which they had thought was protected. The owner barely inquired about what we had gone through. I was the one who asked him whether he had family in Beirut. A daughter, whose house was slightly damaged, he replied distractedly. We were quiet, suddenly, and the immemorial silence settled in for a few moments. The summits around us were gleaming and looking away, indifferent to our pains, as they have been for millennia. This is what I've never been able to make my children understand about my fascination with these landscapes that I've carried since childhood: the mountains' silence, this immense peace, as if they were the last witnesses of what must have been the planet's eternal stasis before time and history burst in, and before the disorder, ruin, and entropy that human beings have unceasingly wreaked, ever since they started to writhe upon the Earth.

70

August 17

When I found out that the little street where Sarah lives was severely damaged, I remembered an old friend of my mother's whom I hadn't heard from for years. She had always lived on this street, although I didn't know whether she was still living there, at her advanced age. The landline on which I tried to call her was obviously out of order, and I no longer had the numbers of any of her daughters. I went over there yesterday afternoon. The building was badly hit, there are no more windows, the elevator shaft is gaping open, all the doors have been ripped off, the handrail in the stairwell has come adrift, on each of the landings you can see inside the homes and through to the street on the other side, and as you go up the floors, you can see the port and the sky at last. But at every level, everything has been cleared out, tidied up, put away. Whatever could be saved was set aside, the rest was in a heap ready to be taken away, thanks to the teams of young volunteers.

There were lots of people on the floor where my mother's old friend lived. A team of volunteer architects working for an NGO was surveying the damage to the walls, the ceilings, the facade. Maya, one of the daughters of the owner, was there too. She reassured me about her mother, who doesn't stay at the apartment much anymore, because she can no longer walk, and lives with another one of her children. She showed me around the apartment, where after the cleanup there were still a few pieces of old furniture, including an immovable sideboard, an intact chandelier hanging in an empty room, and a couch in the middle of the living room, turned toward the gaping facade. She opened the sideboard, in which there was a complete set of crystal glasses, undamaged.

One of the architects recognized me and said that he was sure I would have a few things to say about all this. We chatted, with his colleagues too. One of them said he had seen one of those agents that everyone is talking about who discreetly go through neighborhoods making despicable offers to the impoverished inhabitants, on behalf of promoters and speculators, to buy up their destroyed homes. Another one told me how, two days after the explosion, a caterer had sent his deliverymen to collect the plates in which he had supplied food to his customers in the last days before the catastrophe, clearly concerned only that his soup tureens and sauce boats had been blasted away with the rest of the city. As we were talking, I had sat down with Maya on the couch, in front of the gaping facade, looking out into the open space as if we were sitting on a balcony above the sea and the ruins of the port, which you couldn't quite see from inside.

At one point, one of the architects came and offered me a piece of chocolate, from one of those mass-produced bars that have a cream filling with chemical fruit flavors and colors, and you wonder how they can still be available for sale, given how long it's been since they can no longer compete with other products that are similar but less bad. It was all that was left from the candy display of a little grocer on the street, who was now working from the sidewalk while waiting for his store to be usable again. I don't know if the young architect, who was apologizing for having nothing else to offer us, noticed how touched and satisfied I was, but those chocolate bars are the ones we used to have when we were children, in the mountains. They were the only ones available at the time in the isolated villages, and as I bit into the thin outside layer covering the artificial cream, I knew it would happen, and it did: I fleetingly saw my childhood summers, the gleaming solitary mountains, my cousins and their friends, the bicycle races, the picnics under the walnut trees, the cold water from the spring, the endless games of Risk, and the cool fog that gradually lifts in the afternoon.

71

August 18

Covid-19 took the opportunity of our being distracted with other things to come back with a vengeance. The case numbers are rising again, and a new lockdown, which no one had talked about for a while, is now imminent. Our money is still being held hostage by the banks, we're starting to wonder whether it even exists anymore, we barter and do business with checks or credit cards, or with bundles of national currency that have little value anymore. Inflation, which had been rising slowly, stealthily, in the previous months, has now exploded in our face. This makes things very complicated for those who are rebuilding or restoring their houses at their own cost, as well as for the countless organizations that are helping those worst off to do so, thanks to international support. The enemy is legion, and at its head is the oligarchy in power, with its interests, its accounts, and its fearsome survival instinct. It hasn't changed its modus operandi one iota since the disaster, it is still ransacking the moribund public coffers and is in no hurry to form a new government. We are under siege, but from the inside. *The government is trying to overthrow the people.*

72

August 19

As if in response, this morning, on a few badly damaged facades in the Mar Mikhaël district where I was passing with Saria, red and white banners have been hung up: NOUS NE PARTIRONS PAS, NOUS RECONSTRUIRONS—WE WILL NEVER LEAVE, WE WILL REBUILD—لن نرحل سنعيد بناء بيروت

73

'm writing these lines while sitting on the terrace. It's very hot but a breeze has risen up and is blowing without conviction. In its gusts an empty drink can is rolling down the quiet street, bouncing along with a joyful clatter, sometimes soft, sometimes loud, like the little tinkling bells on a poor herd of mountain goats, and then it disappears, blown away.

74

don't know why, but I remember what Ronald Moussa told me three weeks ago—in other words in another era, before the explosion. He was having dinner with his wife, on the waterfront at Amchit. They were sitting at the very end of the jetty, directly above the water. He had put a cigar down on the table, which the wind had discreetly started rolling away, gently playing at pushing it to the edge of the table, where it finally tipped off, just as Ronald, in a leap almost like a survival reflex, as if his life depended on it, and at the risk of tipping over into the water himself, as he later told me and laughed, caught it and prevented it from ending up in the sea.

75

Our lives, like that drink can and that cigar, thrown to the winds...